The Battle of Lepanto

NANAMI SHIONO

Translated by
Carolyn L. Temporelli, Steven Bryan and Wilburn Hansen

Published by Vertical, Inc., New York.

Originally published in Japanese as *Repanto no Kaisen* by Shinchosha, Tokyo, 1987.

ISBN 1-932234-33-0/978-1-932234-33-6

Manufactured in the United States of America

First American Edition

Vertical, Inc.
1185 Avenue of the America 32nd Floor
New York, NY 10036
www.vertical-inc.com

Paul VI was Pope, so it must have been ten years ago. I was watching the Italian state news and couldn't help but smile when I heard the following report:

> As an expression of his desire to establish friendly relations with peoples of other faiths, Pope Paul VI has decided to give the Islamic battle flag captured by the Christian fleet in the 1571 Battle of Lepanto back to Turkey. The Pope handed the flag today to the Turkish ambassador to Italy.

I realize that, regardless of place or time, having one's flag captured by the enemy has always been considered an extreme humiliation, but the Battle of Lepanto took place over four hundred years ago.

The Military Museum in Istanbul contains spoils of war from various Christian countries; the street in front is lined with cannons taken as trophies of war from the army of the former Republic of Venice. The modern-day Turkish Republic doesn't display these items captured three or four hundred years ago out of pride, however. After the passage of so much time they are no longer the spoils of war but, rather, historical relics.

Turkey must have wondered what to do with that flag. Turkish schoolbooks still don't mention the Ottoman defeat at Lepanto, and there is no greater proof of defeat than a battle flag captured by the enemy. I doubt the Turks would want to display the flag prominently, but they also cannot simply burn something that was returned to them in a spirit of goodwill.

I am certain that this bothersome object was stowed in the back of some archive because, after I watched that broadcast, I traveled to Turkey and searched for it extensively without success. I scoured Topkapi Palace as well as the Military Museum, which contains memorabilia from all of the Ottoman Empire's battles on both land and sea. I even looked in the Naval Museum, which seems to be perennially closed, but in the end never found the flag.

The flag was made of white silk and embroidered in gold with a verse from the Koran. It had been brought especially for the Battle of Lepanto from the holy land of Mecca and flown from the mast of the flagship of the Ottoman navy's grand admiral, Ali Pasha.

Now, thanks to the work of self-styled "progressive" idealists, we have lost the opportunity to ever see it again. I doubt that many people today, four hundred years later, are led to believe that Christians are superior to Muslims by seeing that flag in the Vatican Museum. I also cannot believe that the number of Muslims who would be offended is significant.

The Battle of Lepanto was a single historical event. While it does have a certain distinctiveness as a battle between Christians and Muslims, as in all other wars the outcome was ultimately decided by how the men on each side fought. In that sense, it makes no difference that it was fought by Christians and Muslims, or even that it took place four hundred years ago.

The Battle of Lepanto marked the end of the long age in which the Mediterranean Sea was history's stage, and it was also the final great battle in which galley warships played the leading role.

Next door to my study (which I call my "archives"), there is a long, thin room, at the center of which is a desk that has been covered for several months with a chart. When this chart, which measures one meter by seventy centimeters, is lined up with a 1:10,000 scale map made by the British navy of the seas around Lepanto, the two essentially cover all of the desk, a medieval monastery desk that measures two hundred and forty by seventy centimeters. A 1:1,000,000 scale map made by the Italian navy that depicts all of the Aegean Sea from Southern Italy to Greece barely peeks out from beneath the other two.

The chart lists the more than four hundred Christian and Muslim ships that participated in the Battle of Lepanto, although for some ships nothing but the ensign, name, nationality, and captain's name are recorded. I cut the chart out of a scholarly book published in Venice half a century ago, to which it was the appendix. I bought the volume in a used bookstore several years ago not because I was interested in the text but because I wanted the chart.

The paper on which the chart is printed was probably of good quality in its day. After fifty years, however, and even though it had not been read by many people, the paper had a yellow tint, the lettering in the creases had faded away, and the chart had been torn in four places. My first task was to trace over the faded letters in pencil and to reinforce the ripped portions with transparent cellophane tape.

The chart is divided down the middle with the Christian warships to the left and the Muslim warships to the right so that they face each other. The ships from the various Christian countries are listed with the left flank at the top, the main force in the middle and the right flank at the bottom, while the rear guard is lined up on the far left edge. Similarly, the formation of the Muslim fleet shows the right flank at the top, the main force in the middle, and then the left flank at the bottom. It thus depicts the precise alignment of the ships immediately before the two fleets clashed at the mouth of the Gulf of Patras near noon on October 7, 1571.

I would like to point out a few particular entries. The top of the chart lists the war galley that was positioned on the far left side of the left flank of the Christian formation:

> 1. Flagship of the navy of the Venetian Republic. Commander of the left flank, Admiral Agostino Barbarigo. Ship's captain, Federico Nani. Commander of the knights, Sigismondo Malatesta. Commander of the foot soldiers, Silvio de Portia.

Securing the corresponding far right flank of the Muslim forces we find:

> I. Egyptian flagship. Commander, Governor of Alexandria, Mohammed Suluk.

Few people would be able to tell on the basis of this entry alone, but this governor of Alexandria was in fact also known as "Scirocco" (southeastern wind). He was best known by this nickname, and his primary occupation was in fact that of pirate captain.

Unlike Venice, Turkey was not a maritime nation and had no heritage of naval warfare. It thus had to rely on Muslim pirates when forming its navy. These pirates were appointed as governors and pashas in places such as Alexandria, Tunis, and Algiers, known dens of piracy. In return, they were called upon to serve whenever the Ottoman Empire fought at sea. This system benefited not only the Ottoman sultan but the pirate leaders as well: regardless of their power, the pirates had always been considered outcasts. This system gave them official recognition.

The ship securing the furthest edge of the Muslim fleet's left flank appears at the bottom of the right side of the chart:

> 246. Algerian flagship. Captain, King Uluch Ali of Algeria, commander of the Muslim navy's left flank.

Uluch Ali was also a pirate captain. But unlike the others, who were all Arab or Greek, he happened to be an Italian born Giovanni Galeni in southern Italy. He had been kidnapped by pirates as a boy and had spent several years as a galley slave but now commanded the Muslim fleet's left flank. It was customary to entrust the two flanks of a fleet to experienced naval commanders; as these examples show, in the Muslim fleet these key positions were occupied by veteran pirates.

The Christian forces also secured their flanks with experienced sea captains. A commander from Genoa, whose maritime tradition rivaled that of Venice, led the right flank facing Uluch Ali. The Venetian Agostino Barbarigo protected the far left flank.

> 167. The Doria fleet flagship. Captain, Gian Andrea Doria, commander of the Christian fleet's right flank. On board, Vincenzo Carafa, Octavio Gonzaga, and numerous other knights and nobles.

This ship is listed on the bottom of the chart's left half. The chart doesn't say so, but Doria was not in fact an admiral of the Genoese Republic's navy. He was exclusively the commander of the Doria family fleet, which he led from that fleet's flagship. The members of the Doria family were mercenary captains whose ships, sailors, and even soldiers were available for hire. The patron of the

Doria family at the time of the Battle of Lepanto was King Philip II of Spain. Incidentally, the Genoese Republic's flagship stayed with the main Christian fleet, where the flagships of various countries were centered. It is listed as follows:

> 84. Genoese fleet flagship. Captain, Etolle Spinola. On board, Duke Alexandro Falnuze.

It is only natural to wonder how the ship of the supreme commander of the Christian fleet is described. Unfortunately, that entry is in the center of the chart, where the paper is most badly damaged. It is not only yellowed and weakened but is also torn along the crease, making the writing difficult to decipher. Close inspection, however, reveals the following:

> 86. Flagship of the Christian Alliance. Captain, Juan Vasquez de Coronado. On board, Supreme Commander of the Allied Fleet of the Holy League, Austrian Duke Don Juan.

One hundred attendants were aboard, including thirty-eight Spanish nobles and Don Juan's personal confessor priest Francisco, who was especially appointed by Philip II. In addition, there were four hundred carefully selected musketmen from Sardinia.

Adjacent to this large war galley are the flagships of the Venetian Republic and the Papal States, the two other main participants in the anti-Turkish alliance:

> 85. Flagship of the Venetian Republic navy.
> Commander, Admiral Sebastiano Veniero.
> 87. Flagship of the Papal States Navy. Captain,
> Gaspar Bruni. On board, Duke Marcanto-
> nio Colonna, Lieutenant Supreme Com-
> mander of the Holy League Fleet. Also on
> board, Pope Pius V's nephew, Paolo Gisrieli,
> and numerous other Roman nobles. Also 25
> Swiss Guards, 180 foot soldiers, and
> numerous volunteer knights from France.

It is clear at a glance that the above ships carried the fleet's top commanders, but ordinary warships are typically described on the chart in the following manner:

> 123. Flag, Image of the resurrected Christ.
> Venice. Captain, Benedetto Solanzo.
> 33. Ship name, La Marquesa. Doria fleet.
> Captain, Francisco Sanfedra.

The young Miguel de Cervantes served as a soldier on this last galley.

Although the chart records only the dry facts, it is not difficult to imagine that every man aboard those ships experienced his own personal drama. It would be difficult to flesh out those stories, however, without resorting to complete fabrication.

According to Anatole France, history is an enumeration of notable facts. Although something may be factual, it risks not being treated as history if it is not noteworthy. Without doubt, Cervantes's participation in the Battle of Lepanto would have gone unnoticed had he not later written *Don Quixote*. Writing a history from the perspective of the common man is easier said than done.

The second thing I did during the long months I spent studying this chart was to underline the names of the captains and commanders who, according to other historical sources, died during the battle. I was stunned by just how large the number of deaths was. Yet this exercise was useful as a visual indication of where the battle was fiercest.

It would be another two hundred years or more before sea battles evolved into the lobbing of cannon balls back and forth between distant ships, as at the Battle of Trafalgar. At the time of the Battle of Lepanto, so-called sea battles merely meant that the fighting occurred at sea. This was close-quarter combat using swords, spears, guns, and bows and arrows as soldiers moved from one ship to another. In that sense, it hardly differed from combat on land. The distribution of deaths among the commanding officers thus accurately indicates where the fighting was most intense.

Who was it who said that politics is war without bloodshed while war is politics with bloodshed? Mao

Zedong? Clausewitz? Both? If there is any truth to this idea, before I describe the politics that sheds blood, I must first describe the war that doesn't.

The Battle of Lepanto started out as such a bloodless war, then turned into a bloody politics and at last reverted to the bloodless war. It might be said that other wars are no different.

Venice – Autumn 1569

Agostino Barbarigo left the Palazzo Ducale earlier that day than usual.

He had completed his two-year assignment in Cyprus and had returned to Venice a week earlier. He had been too busy reporting to the senate and the Council of Ten, however, to relax at the home from which he had for so long been separated.

Venetian high officials were worried that they had not correctly grasped the Ottoman Empire's intentions toward Cyprus, and Barbarigo's return provided a welcome opportunity to find out more. Since Barbarigo had returned home after serving a tour of predetermined length, questioning him now would not alarm the Turks the way that recalling him home would have. Even after the standard debriefing, the senators and members of the Council, wanting to know his views, continued pressing him with questions. For many days the questioning continued well after the lamps in the senate chamber had been lit.

Barbarigo, however, was not distressed that all he had seen since his return was the route between his home on the Grand Canal and the palace. Born into the most aristocratic of the noble families, his sense of responsibility to Venice was as natural to him as the blood flowing through his veins.

His wife, who was also born into an aristocratic Venetian family, managed without her husband in style.

He was away more often than not, and his return after long absences did not affect her social engagements. They had no children, and his nephew, whom they had adopted, was serving as the ambassador's deputy in England, which was then under the reign of Elizabeth I.

The soft, warm evening light enveloped his whole body as he left the palace and went out to the docks of San Marco. There wasn't a single ripple in the sea stretching out before him. Gondolas were moored at the dock waiting to take government officials home after they had finished work. Many of the elderly councilors liked to travel by gondola from the palace to their front door.

Not surprisingly, Barbarigo felt a great sense of relief as he basked in the soft sunlight: he was finally free of the continuous days of questioning. His next assignment, though, would almost certainly be handed down without delay. Under no circumstances would the Venetian government of that time allow a man like him—who for two years had been the naval commander of Cyprus, Venice's outermost territory—simply to relax.

Barbarigo knew that full well. He had nonetheless decided to spend what few days of freedom he had been granted at his villa on the Venetian mainland. The thought of spending time at that villa, which was surrounded by farmland and filled with various memories from his youth, brought a smile to his face.

There was one thing he had to do before departing, however. A certain issue had been bothering him for the past two years, and it was only now that he had the time to address it. It was the reason why he had left the palace from the door opposite the one he would have normally used to go home.

He planned to visit the aristocratic home of his former lieutenant. According to the reports he had received, the house was located in the San Severo parish, far from the area along the Grand Canal where most of the rich and noble families of Venice resided.

Walking with a firm gait with the evening sun at his back, Barbarigo crossed the bridge that divided the continuous dock into San Marco and Riva degli Schiavoni. The fleet's flagships had dropped their anchors at a pier along San Marco, while the battleships were aligned at a pier along Riva degli Schiavoni. When these docks weren't occupied by war galleys, they were filled with endless rows of merchant ships.

This extensive port was long ago named Riva degli Schiavoni, which means "Bank of the Dalmatians," a sign of respect for the Dalmatian region that supplied the sailors indispensable for both the warships and merchant vessels of the maritime state of Venice.

Many low-ranking sailors who served on Venetian ships lived in this area. There were even Orthodox Greek churches. As he walked along the bank of the Riva degli Schiavoni, Barbarigo briefly wondered why a Venetian nobleman would live in such a district. That was the extent of the thought he gave to the matter, however, since Venice wasn't neatly divided into "wealthy" and "common" neighborhoods. Even along the Grand Canal, all you could say was that there were more wealthy homes than on other stretches.

Barbarigo crossed another of Venice's uniquely arched bridges. He smiled wryly as it occurred to him that his long time abroad had made him forget just how it felt to cross these spaces.

Agostino Barbarigo's height was not conspicuous when he was among Venetian nobles, who were generally tall. He stood out, however, among merchants from the Orient or the Dalmatian and Greek-born ship hands and oarsmen who thronged the Riva degli Schiavoni, his head being the only one poking above the crowd. The black wool robe he wore during senate meetings further accentuated his height.

He was in his mid-forties. His hair, still mostly black and rich, was cut short in a mass of tight curls, which allowed him to don his steel helmet more easily. A black beard covered the lower half of his face, but as with his hair, gray was creeping in. He styled the tip of his beard into a triangle, which proved that he was not completely indifferent to appearances. It also imparted severity to his typically long Venetian face. His eyes were a deep, calm blue. His tanned, light brown complexion was the single feature distinguishing him from the government officials who until recently had been bombarding him with questions.

He carried nothing, as he had previously arranged

delivery of the dead lieutenant's personal effects. It had become Barbarigo's custom, if given the opportunity, to visit the homes of those who had died in battle under his command, or at least those of the officers.

He proceeded down the Riva degli Schiavoni for a while and then turned left into an alley. This road ran in front of the Church of San Zaccaria, and while it would take him out of his way, the extra distance didn't amount to much. For some reason he had been fond of this church since childhood. In truth, the church's façade appealed to him more than the church itself.

The Church of San Zaccaria stood forever quiet. Its well-curved form, which seemed somehow foreign though it was of a sort seen only in Venice, was free of all excess. The structure projected a purifying calm, perhaps because it was made entirely of white marble. Whenever Barbarigo looked at the church's façade, it filled him with a sense of both tranquility and light-heartedness.

Although the piazza in front of the Church of San Zaccaria was less than twenty meters from the Riva degli Schiavoni, it was strangely insulated from the noise of the docks. It was not that there were no passers-by, rather that its layout was different from those of Venice's other piazzas. In the others, one passed from alley to alley and crossed the square at an angle, but here one passed through only one side of the square while seeing the church's façade out of the corner of one's eye. This remoteness from the human world was probably why the church exuded such a sense of calm. It was impossible to find this sort of feeling with any other Venetian church, except in the dead of night when all were asleep.

Barbarigo stopped when he entered the piazza. The white marble covering the church's front was bathed in the evening sun and took on a warm hue. Perhaps because it was not time for Mass, there was no one around except a lone beggar curled up by the church's entrance. Barbarigo stood in front of this familiar scene steeped in the sense of finally having come home. The cathedral doors opened at that moment and a young boy appeared, immediately followed by a woman.

The beggar seemed to have been sleeping, but he had been roused, and called out to them. The woman had intended to pass, but she now stopped. She whispered to the boy at her side and gave him something that appeared to be loose change from the small bag in her hand. The boy approached the beggar, bent down, and handed it to him—he didn't throw it. The boy returned to the woman, who was waiting a few steps away, and the two walked off toward an alley opposite where Barbarigo stood.

They were no doubt mother and son. One could see the intimacy in the way the woman whispered to the boy, and in the way he replied. Without their even noticing it, that intimacy had grown over time into the tenderness that only comes from mutual understanding. Barbarigo felt overwhelmed by a sense of longing. It had been ages since he had experienced that emotion.

He knew at a glance that the mother was not Venetian.

Venetian-born women were generally voluptuous, with golden-red hair. Even those who weren't naturally blonde went to great lengths to lighten their hair by baking it in the sun, a style they called "Venetian blonde." Although this woman covered her hair with a thin, black veil, it was clearly black. Her body was different too, thin and supple. Compared with most Venetian women, who walked with heavy, lumbering steps, her stride had an elegant lightness.

The boy was perhaps ten years old. He had a lithe frame like his mother, but his musculature was still that of a child. Barbarigo smiled at the way he spoke to her. Following closely at her heels, he seemed like a puppy being walked by its owner. He talked continuously, even when he fell a few paces behind her. Perhaps he was compensating for the imposed silence of the church. He jumped from one topic to another as he looked up at his mother's face. She gently answered each question, never breaking her stride.

Mother and son passed through an alley leading away from the piazza. The alley from San Zaccaria's Piazza seemed to go right under the building, so the phrase "passed through" is quite appropriate. After emerging from the alley, which was carved with a relief of the Virgin Mary, the two took the road to the right.

Barbarigo was also taking that road, so he followed

behind them. He trailed twenty or thirty steps back; he wanted to savor that sense of gentle nostalgia that came from looking at them. They didn't seem to notice Barbarigo at all.

After some time they came out onto a canal. Although they were still on the same path, it now followed the canal and was thus called a *fondamenta*, or dock support, rather than simply a *calle*, or pathway. Venice was crisscrossed with canals and boats were everywhere, so any path where a boat could pull alongside functioned not only as a road, but also as a dock.

After following the sidewalk a short way along the canal, they came to a small bridge. The mother and son began to cross the bridge while still carrying on their exchange. Barbarigo remembered that, in order to reach the San Severo parish, he too needed to cross a bridge in this area. This side of the river was the San Zaccaria parish; San Severo parish was on the other bank.

Barbarigo had been a couple of dozen paces behind the woman and child, but once he reached the arched bridge, they were nowhere to be seen. They were neither on the bridge nor on the straight road that stretched on ahead. It wasn't that they had vanished into a crowd; the area was a considerable distance from the city center, and other than the local residents there were rarely passersby. He saw only a cat creeping through the dark, bleak alley where the late-day sun couldn't penetrate.

Barbarigo sighed. He felt that something like a black curtain had cut him off from the pleasing scene of mother and son. But it also reminded him of his original objective. A small, white marble address plaque posted on the door of the house beside him caught his eye.

The city of Venice is divided into six administrative regions called *sestere*, and each *sestere* is subdivided into several regions called parishes. Accordingly, each house address in Venice is composed of the house number, the parish, and the *sestere*.

Since Venice is not on the mainland and space is limited, people use every available inch. The number of different names for paved surfaces, such as *piazza* (plaza), *campo* (square), *corte* (open ground), *carre* (streets), *viccolo* (paths), *fondamenta* (sidewalks), and *sotto portico* (side streets), attests to their wide and diverse usage. Other cities follow ancient Roman conventions of naming streets; Venice doesn't have that luxury. While other cities use addresses with house numbers and street names, such a notational system is impossible in Venice. Even today, the city's system remains unchanged, making it difficult to locate addresses.

Barbarigo was having difficulty finding the address he was looking for. Among the houses packed tightly together in this area was the mansion of the Priuli family, eminent even among Venice's aristocracy. The address was only one digit different from the one Barbarigo was searching for. He knocked at their front gate to ask directions. A servant politely told him that the house he was looking for was right behind the Priuli residence and explained how to get there.

Barbarigo finally arrived at the entrance of his destination. A tree nearly completely covered it from sight, and for the first time it struck him: land was so precious in Venice that, although there were separate entrances, even well-known nobles' houses commonly backed into other homes. The building code allowed the city to house the many people who came to Venice because of its flourishing foreign trade. The house Barbarigo had at last found was one of the rental properties meant to do just that.

There was a small metal bell to announce visitors; it was hanging above his head in the shadow of the yellow foliage of the tree. Barbarigo hesitantly rang it. After a while the door opened a crack. Still standing outside, Barbarigo explained the reason for his visit. He remained outside as the woman in her fifties who had answered the door went to inform her mistress. He pondered the old woman's strong Tuscan accent as he waited.

She returned and ushered him in, this time opening the gate fully. Yellow leaves fell without end into the courtyard, a space too small even to be called a garden. A stone stairway on one side led up to the second floor, where there was an open door that marked the entrance to the house proper. The woman passed through the foyer, led Barbarigo through one small room, and opened the door to a room where she instructed him to wait. Then she vanished.

The room seemed to be for greeting visitors. It was not large, but there were two southern-facing windows overlooking a canal. The buildings in Venice were not blessed with good sunlight because of the narrow canals and because four- or five-story buildings were placed right next to each other—adjacent buildings often protruded directly in front of one's eyes. The current room, however, was neither dim nor gloomy.

A half-circular fireplace was cut out of one corner, but no fire was burning. This upper floor, as well as the floors above it, were probably used for the living quarters. Though the rooms were quite small, the southern exposure and canal view made them quite pleasant compared to those of other houses in Venice. There was no doubt, though, that it was rather small. The furnishings and fixtures in the room caught Agostino Barbarigo's attention. They were not only Florentine, but also of considerably high quality.

The house was quiet inside, without a sound. Barbarigo briefly even forgot that he was being made to wait. He stood by the slightly open window, looking aimlessly down at the canal. He sensed someone approach and turned to find a woman, dressed in pale blue, standing in the room's entrance.

At that moment Barbarigo did something normally unimaginable for him. As soon as he realized who the woman was, he completely forgot his usual habit of greeting people with an elegant bow. Instead he stepped confidently toward her, took her hands, and covered them in his own. The woman's delicate, lightly made-up face didn't show any surprise either. She only smiled warmly.

That moment, in which these two strangers were no longer strangers, came and went with uncanny spontaneity.

They sat down and Barbarigo began in a quiet voice to tell the woman the circumstances of her husband's death two years earlier. She listened quietly and calmly without shedding a tear.

A bullet fired by a Turkish soldier had struck him down in a sea battle near Cyprus. News of his death was immediately sent to his family, but since there was no way to prevent putrefaction during the long sea voyage back to the Venetian Republic, the bodies of war dead were not returned to their homeland. The standard protocol was to bury them at the nearest Venetian outpost. Citizens of the republic were buried in cemeteries on Cyprus, Crete, and even Corfu, which was only ten days by ship from Venice. Thus, most families were never able to see the remains of their loved ones. Even if a grave was laid in Venice, most didn't even contain a lock of the deceased's hair.

Outside the room, the old woman said something. Inside the room, it had become completely dark. The woman asked her servant, who had brought in candles, to call in her son. She then asked Barbarigo if he could repeat to her son the story that he had just told her. Of course, he didn't object.

Not surprisingly, the mood in the room changed

completely when the boy entered. He smiled playfully and, after making a dutifully polite greeting, sat down in front of the visitor. Barbarigo repeated the same story, but his tone and manner of telling had changed to that of one grown man addressing another. This was due, in part, to the fact that he had no son of his own and did not know how to speak to children. But he also had no desire to treat even a ten-year-old as a child when telling him of his father's death. The boy responded with the maturity that had been expected of him. He listened intently, with the calm composure of an adult.

The mother sat slightly apart from the other two, looking on as the story was retold in this way. Her face showed no sadness. Rather, as if she were remembering a warmth whose very existence she had long since forgotten, her face glowed with gentle happiness.

After leaving the woman's house, Barbarigo boarded a gondola at the foot of the bridge. He told the gondolier the name of his residence and sank into a small chair in the cabin lined with black wool. As the small boat glided over the water, he allowed his heart to fill with warm memories. Any thought of going to his villa in the outskirts of the city had completely disappeared.

Constantinople – Autumn 1569

Everyone thought Marcantonio Barbaro was well over seventy years old when they first met him. Although he was in fact a dozen years younger than that, he bore every possible sign of age.

First, he was as thin as a crane. Though tall, his body seemed like muscle and bone wrapped in a layer of tanned skin without an ounce of fat in between. His brow was bald, and what little hair remained hung intertwined with his beard. Most of his hair had now turned from black to white and was completely unkempt, appearing from a distance like a wild mass of gray. His face had been etched with layer upon layer of wrinkles, and although his nose was thin, one could not help but notice its hawk-like shape. That and his glinting, piercing eyes left no doubt that this was no ordinary old man, an impression that was only strengthened if one actually spoke with him. Those who understood that his physical transformation was largely due to his service as the Venetian ambassador to Turkey must have considered his birth in a country that valued diplomats so highly the only redeeming aspect of his plight.

Barbaro had been stationed in Constantinople for a little over a year, since August 1568. It would never occur to him that his stay would last for five years, much less that three of those would be spent in captivity.

His prior ambassadorial posting had been in the court of the powerful nation of France. While not even fellow Christian countries could be trusted at that time, Turkey was a special case for Venice, as both countries' interests collided head on in the Eastern Mediterranean. It was customary for the Venetian Republic to send its most veteran ambassadors, those with prior diplomatic experience in France or Spain, to Turkey.

This had been the case with Barbaro, who the Venetian senate felt was the best card they held when tensions with Turkey began to mount. The selection was not surprising, since Barbaro was the kind of person who could quickly grasp a situation upon arrival at a new post. He once wrote the following in a report he sent back to Venice: "Diplomatic negotiations with Turkey are like playing catch with a glass ball. The other side may throw the ball hard, but we cannot return it with the same force, nor can we allow the ball to be dropped."

No wonder he looked ten years older than he really was.

An assignment to Turkey, Venice's primary potential enemy, guaranteed that a diplomat would have enough worries to produce a wrinkle per month, even in peacetime. Since signs had emerged that the Turks planned to throw the glass ball harder than usual this year, the autumn of 1569 seemed to Barbaro to be more like winter.

A fire broke out at the Venetian national *arsenale*, or shipyard, on September 13th of that year. The *arsenale* was not only a shipyard; it was a kind of mass assembly line where everything from fitting the hull and planks to launching the finished boat was done in a single, unified process. It also contained warehouses where ships could be outfitted with cannons, as well as firearms and cross-bows for foot soldiers. There were also facilities to assemble sails, and even large stores of gunpowder. For this reason, it was located far from the center of town in the northeastern part of Venice. In a city where castle walls were otherwise completely absent, it was the only locale surrounded by a high fortress wall.

The fire that broke out late on the night of September 13th turned into a conflagration when it spread to three of the gunpowder arsenals, which then exploded. There were four explosions that not only reduced 14,000 ducats worth of gunpowder to ash, but also blasted a nearly forty-meter hole in the nearby fortress wall. The convent and church next door were also destroyed. The damage to the ships, however, was minor, as only four galleys were burned.

The citizens of Venice knew of the shipyard's gun-powder arsenals. Fearing the possibilities, they fled their quarters until dawn in boats that jammed Venice's canals as far away as the Grand Canal. The only stroke of good fortune was that no additional flames reached the gun-powder warehouses and that just a few days earlier 240,000 librae of gunpowder, which had been stored near the fire's origin, had been sent to Corfu. Several dozen galleys under construction were also largely unharmed.

Workers quickly repaired the areas damaged by the fire and explosions. The shipyard returned to business as usual in less than a week. It generally took a month, however, for information from Venice to reach Constantinople. News favorable to the Turks, however, somehow managed to arrive faster. The Turkish court thus learned of the fire soon after the event but did not know of the subsequent rebuilding until much later.

The hardliners in the Turkish court took action immediately upon hearing the first reports. Convinced that the Venetian fleet could not recover, they insisted that now was the time to reclaim Cyprus and Crete. The moderate faction, which until this point had successfully contained the hardliners, saw its position grow tenuous.

The moderates at that time were still faithful to the ideas of the former sultan, Suleiman, who had died three years earlier. The faction's current leader was the Grand Vizier Sokullu, the only high Turkish official with whom Venetian Ambassador Barbaro felt he could negotiate. The moderates—as is always the case—were realists. They believed that the Venetian Republic's economic strength helped Turkey to manage the Ottoman Empire.

The Venetians had no wish to extend their territory. What they needed was the freedom to pursue their economic activities, and both Cyprus and Crete were important for this. Meanwhile, Turkey controlled a vast domain surrounding the Eastern Mediterranean. The moderates in the Turkish court thus felt that their polity's interests coincided, in fact, with those of the Venetian Republic. They could see no reason to wage war on Venice.

Conversely, the hardliners led by Piali Pasha consolidated their position with the addition of newcomers to the court that surrounded the new sultan, Selim. This faction, in short, was a collection of idealists who believed in the basic tenets of Islam and the necessity of spreading the Koran's teachings throughout the world. For them, leaving Christian outposts within their empire was nothing short of a humiliation. At the same time, they had no conception of what recovering Cyprus and Crete would actually contribute to the Ottoman Empire. The yearly fees Venice paid for use of Cyprus provided more economic benefit than Turkey's direct rule ever would, but this carried absolutely no weight with the hardliners. Turkey was a massive empire, one that surpassed even Spain, and driving Christians from the Eastern Mediterranean was a matter of honor.

The young Sultan Selim's only talent was drinking, even though he was the son of the man the whole world exalted as "Suleiman the Magnificent." When sober, Selim was a tyrant who toyed with the ambition of doing something even his father had never attempted.

The Venetian government sent Ambassador Barbaro accurate information on the shipyard fire. In fact, there was no one in Constantinople with more accurate knowledge of the damage.

Barbaro decided that it was to his advantage to disclose everything he knew to Grand Vizier Sokullu. He went to Topkapi Palace with only an interpreter and gave the grand vizier a complete account of what had happened, from the particulars of which ships had received what damage, to the time and money needed for the repairs. This information was meant to help the moderates recover their influence.

Calming the already inflamed emotions in the Turkish court, however, would prove more difficult than it had been to extinguish the fire in the shipyard. The hardliners refused to yield to the grand vizier's arguments, giving reason after reason. They argued that pirates in the Aegean Sea attacked Turkish merchant ships because Venetian patrol boats refused to protect Turkish vessels, and that Cyprus had given safe harbor to a ship from the Knights of St. John whose only purpose was to attack Turkish vessels.

These were all baseless accusations. But they unfortunately enjoyed the tacit approval of the all-powerful sultan. Ambassador Barbaro, who had never been lax in his intelligence gathering, became even more passionate about it now. He decided that he had no alternative but to send a warning to his home government. On November 11th, he sent a message that Turkish policy was moving in a dangerous direction. Then, in his report dated December 19th, he confirmed and offered specific proofs of the impending threat. His report can be summarized as follows:

The pace of ship construction is greater than usual at all Turkish ports.

Ship construction is particularly active in ports facing the Mediterranean Sea.

A reliable source has reported that this increased activity is to provide ships for an attack on Cyprus.

He has therefore sent letters to the commanders in Cyprus and Crete urging them to prepare their defenses.

Ambassador Barbaro urged the Venetian government to increase emergency military preparations and to send auxiliary forces to both islands, especially Cyprus. Because Cyprus had been a Venetian colony for more than a hundred years, only police were usually stationed there.

The Byzantine Empire, also known as the Eastern Roman Empire, collapsed in 1453. Constantinople, which from that year forward became the capital of the victorious Turks, was divided by the Golden Horn into the districts of Constantinople and Pera (also known as Galata).

Under the Byzantine Empire, Genoese had been the sole merchants in Pera while Venetians and other Western Europeans were clustered along the shore of the Golden Horn in Constantinople proper. The Venetians, fierce rivals of the Genoese, were far and away the most successful merchants among the Western Europeans. Both

Venice's embassy and trading house were located along the Golden Horn, and their presence was so dominant that the nearby spice bazaar was commonly known as the "Venetian Bazaar."

This situation changed dramatically after the fall of Constantinople in 1453. The Genoese, who had enjoyed exclusive possession of Galata for several centuries, lost their influence. Venetians and other Western Europeans were forced to emigrate from Constantinople to Galata, which at this time came to be called Pera. The Genoese who decided to remain in Pera thus had to share the land.

Venice's embassy and trading house also moved to Pera. The bazaar was all that remained in Constantinople proper. As a result, the Golden Horn became crammed with skiffs passing over the water like whirligig beetles as they ferried western merchants between Pera and Constantinople.

No western power could match Venice in Constantinople, especially after the decline of the Genoese. Perhaps reflecting this changed balance of power, Venice's embassy now occupied the best location among the western embassies in Pera. Situated near the top of the hill on which Pera lay overlooking the Golden Horn, the Venetian embassy commanded a panoramic view of Constantinople. The building itself, however, was far from extravagant. There was barely enough space for the ambassador (who, as a rule, came without his family), the deputy, the secretary, and the servants, including a cook. The furnishings, too, were no match for those in any

noble home in Venice. This austerity was not due to a lack of funds; the Venetians were merely wary of offending the sultan through any kind of extravagance.

Barbaro looked out of his window in the embassy's most comfortable room out onto Constantinople, which was bathed in the weak winter sunlight. The domed roofs and pointed minarets left no doubt that this was now a Muslim city. It had been a long time since Barbaro had gazed at Constantinople so intently.

He had just sent his emergency report to the Venetian government the previous day, using two separate codes and means of delivery. Now he would have to wait for Venice to act. He still had some unfinished business, however.

He needed to provide measures for the security of Venice's merchants within the Ottoman Empire, and especially those within Constantinople, in case of war. He therefore ordered the Venetian trading houses in Constantinople to import more wheat.

Venice itself was not self-sufficient in terms of food. It relied on imports from Turkey, primarily wheat from the Black Sea region. If these stopped, Venice would be in trouble. Barbaro could increase imports for the time being, but Venice would still need other suppliers. This, however, was the responsibility of the home government. Crete was the only Venetian colony that could produce enough wheat to export. In any case, it was winter now. Barbaro prayed that the current situation would hold at least until the wheat harvest was complete.

Venice – Winter 1569

People do not lack the ability to see the truth. Not infrequently, however, they only see what they want to see. The Venetian government's immediate reaction to Ambassador Barbaro's report is a good example. One cannot say that they possessed insufficient information or that they lacked the will or ability to process that information objectively. Yet the Republic of Venice's response was anything but swift.

Opinion was divided in the senate, which decided Venice's military and diplomatic course. One faction was convinced that Turkey had decided to invade Cyprus, while the other considered the Turks' actions an empty threat meant to raise shipping tariffs—something the Ottoman Empire did quite often.

Under Venice's republican system, the senate functioned by majority vote. The Council of Ten, which deliberated in secret, met when the senate couldn't reach a decision. They, too, were deadlocked on the issue, but at least were able to agree on two things: to hire soldiers to aid Cyprus, and to return the shipyard to full capacity.

A special three-member committee of nobles was formed to oversee the shipyard's progress, with Agostino Barbarigo as chair.

Barbarigo happily accepted this appointment. It gave him a reason to stay in Venice rather than go to his villa in Vicenza.

Every morning he traveled in his personal gondola from his home along the Grand Canal to the shipyard, which his boat had special authorization to enter. He spent his mornings meeting with the chief engineers in his office. Warship production was the main priority, and there were often heated arguments about how best to improve the construction of such ships.

One debate revolved around whether to attach sharpened steel rods to the prows of the battleships. Such rods would serve well to pierce the hulls of enemy vessels.

Another topic was the *galeazza* ("galleass" in English), a hybrid galley and sailing vessel—specifically, where to position the numerous cannons on such ships. The galleasses were the cutting edge in naval warfare at the time, and only the Venetian navy had them.

Barbarigo ate his lunch with the engineers at the shipyard, but his meals were specially delivered fresh from his home, while the engineers and workers spread out the lunches they had brought with them in the morning.

Barbarigo traveled to the nearby home of the widow each day after lunch. He would pick up her son, who had returned from school and finished his own lunch, and return with him to the shipyard to perform his afternoon tasks. The ten-year-old boy seemed to enjoy tagging along while Barbarigo spoke with the engineers during his inspections of the ships. Eyes sparkling, the boy with the still-plump cheeks followed Barbarigo around, boarding ships and looking inside. He would sometimes look up at the tall Barbarigo and shower him with naive questions.

At the sound of the vesper bell, the vast shipyard fell quiet. Barbarigo had developed the habit of walking the boy to his mother's house and then continuing halfway across town to his own home. The boy's mother would sometimes invite him to stay for dinner, and during these occasions Barbarigo witnessed their relatively humble lifestyle. Quite in contrast to the unassuming meals, however, the woman and her son's manners exhibited a dignity that was rare even at the most aristocratic of tables. Over the course of these meals Barbarigo learned many things of which he had known nothing before.

The woman's name was Flora. She had been born and raised in a Florentine family so distinguished that Barbarigo nodded in acknowledgement at the mention of the name. She had met her husband when he was serving as secretary to the Venetian ambassador to Florence. They fell in love, married, and came to live in Venice. The old servant woman had been Flora's nursemaid and had followed her to Venice. Flora's son was born there.

Her husband's parents had two sons. They preferred the second-born, who had married a Venetian nobleman's daughter, over the first, who had married Flora—who was, after all, a foreigner. After Flora's husband died, the second son's family took up residence in the parents' home near the Grand Canal, while she and her son moved into their modest house.

Even if she wanted to, however, Flora couldn't return to her own parents' home in Florence. Her son was a scion of the Venetian aristocracy. He was guaranteed a seat in the republic's legislature at the age of twenty, and at thirty—if he lived that long—he would be eligible for the senate. Furthermore, her parents had already passed away and her older brother had inherited the family home. She had inherited a house in the city of Florence and a villa on the outskirts but had sold them and used the proceeds, along with her wedding dowry, to buy state bonds, the dividends of which provided her with her livelihood. Venice provided no pension for the families of deceased soldiers if they belonged to the aristocracy.

Yet Flora hardly seemed oppressed by her modest surroundings. She firmly stated that the only thing she cared about was raising her son as a Venetian citizen. Her face then relaxed a bit, and she added her thanks to Barbarigo for providing her with the chance to see her son so filled with delight.

Flora was always polite and poised in Barbarigo's presence. There was one occasion, though, when her manner changed in response to something he said. In fact, she fell apart. As they were moving into the salon after dinner, Barbarigo said, "Ships seem to be in perfect condition when cutting through the waves of the sea. Yet even they must at some point enter port for rest and repair. Every ship needs a harbor." Both the boy and the old servant woman were in another room. Only Barbarigo and Flora stood in front of the crackling fire.

Flora's black eyes opened wide and her eyes began to well with tears. A moment later, a single teardrop slid down her cheek. Then the tears began to flow, though she remained silent. Barbarigo clasped her hands in his own, as he had reflexively done when they first met, but this time he didn't let go. After remaining this way for a long time, Barbarigo gently kissed Flora's tear-drenched hands. They tasted faintly of salt.

Barbarigo procured himself a "harbor"—he rented a small house in which to meet Flora. It was away from the center of town, almost midway between Flora's home and the shipyard, to minimize the chance of being seen. He had no difficultly finding a place given the number of rental homes available for foreign merchants passing through the city. It was an extremely small house with only two rooms, but it had a private entrance.

Barbarigo knew how difficult it would have been for Flora to turn her own home into that harbor. While the house she shared with her son and old nursemaid did occupy three floors, one could hardly call it a mansion. There was also the matter of the mood in that house; Flora could not escape her role as mother there.

Without a word, he slipped her a key. He gave her the address, a date, and a time.

Barbarigo waited in the tiny house, so small that one could take in its entirety at a glance. Turning uncharacteristically jittery and out of sorts, he paced the room. He even thought that she might not come. At that moment, he heard fumbling as someone hesitantly inserted a key into an unfamiliar lock. He ran to the door, pulling it open at the precise moment it was pushed open from the outside. She was standing on the other side of the threshold.

Neither said a word. As Barbarigo ushered her in, Flora fell into his arms as naturally as a ship with furled sails glides into harbor. Barbarigo's heart burned with the certainty that here, at last, was a woman who needed him.

Venice – Spring 1570

Only the Venetian Republic regularly sent its warships to patrol the Eastern Mediterranean in peacetime. Even in winter, when other countries typically disarmed, Venice never let down its guard.

In other countries, only merchant ships left port between the start of winter and the following spring. Venice's military ships attempted to sail during those winters when even the merchants stayed in harbor. The ships of most other countries passed the winter either being repaired in shipyards or hoisted on land. The oarsmen, sailors, and many soldiers who manned these warships were normally let go and then rehired in the spring.

Venice was in most respects no different from other countries. The one major exception was this commitment to patrolling the seas with small fleets even in wintertime. The republic needed to maintain a shipyard ready to dispatch ships whenever and wherever the need arose; otherwise its claims to perennial readiness would be nothing more than a charade. Venice's winter patrol boats were deployed even in times of peace (the following numbers doubled between spring and fall, when commercial traffic intensified).

A reserve of ten war galleys waited in Venetian harbors to be dispatched at any time in the northern half of the Adriatic Sea. Six to eight war galleys were also stationed in Corfu at the mouth of the Adriatic to guard southwestern Greece and the southern half of the Adriatic. The commander of this fleet was called the *Capitano del Gulfo*, and no position in the Venetian navy was more important. The Adriatic Sea at the time was referred to as the "Gulf of Venice," and the entrance to this gulf at Corfu was in every sense of the word the gate to the Republic of Venice.

Continuing south from Corfu, the island of Zante came into view, where one large-scale war galley was usually on patrol. Proceeding across the Aegean Sea, one came to the island of Crete, Venice's largest base in the Eastern Mediterranean. Crete was under direct Venetian rule, and even in winter at least four war galleys patrolled this area. The fleet guarding the sea lanes to North Africa was also stationed on Crete.

Further east, in the easternmost reaches of the Mediterranean, was Cyprus. Here too, even in winter, Venice stationed four war galleys because this was the frontline outpost against Turkey. Barbarigo had commanded this fleet until a few months earlier.

Of course, this distribution of sea power was not rigidly maintained. In case of emergency, fleets could be reassigned to the areas where they were most needed. The commander of the fleet at Corfu would take responsibility for leading any such ad hoc joint fleet. In case of full-blown war, however, a naval commander in chief appointed by the Venetian government would take the main fleet from Venice and head south. The commanders of each base fleet, from the commander at Corfu on down, would then answer to the commander in chief, whose official title was simply *Capitano Generale del Mare*.

From 1569 to 1570, the fleets assigned to Corfu, Crete, and Cyprus set out in winter and patrolled until spring, as always. These three islands were also equipped with shipyards outfitted with the best technology and facilities of the time, albeit on a smaller scale than in Venice.

These overseas shipyards continued as usual to accept merchant ships for repairs; the shipyard in Venice itself, however, did not. A newly issued secret order directed the shipyard in Venice to dedicate itself solely to warship construction; private shipyards would handle merchant ship repairs. Barbarigo could thus now focus his attention solely on warships, something he couldn't do on Cyprus.

The ships constructed at the Venetian shipyard during the early spring of 1570 were divided into three broad categories.

First, there were war galleys, commonly called *galera sottile*. They were forty meters long, four meters wide, and measured close to 1.5 meters tall from the water's surface. It was normal for these ships to have one mast onto which a yardarm of some forty meters was attached diagonally. There were a number of large and small sails that were either furled or unfurled depending on the strength of the wind. When winds were favorable, these galleys flew a large, triangular sail.

These ships only had one bridge, at the stern. Though called a bridge, it lacked a fixed roof. Most of these bridges were nothing more than cages draped with the same sturdy fabric used for sails. Battle ships, like racing yachts, are built with a fixed purpose from which nothing can detract; no attention, therefore, was paid to amenities. The prows of the ships had sharpened steel rods attached to them that looked like birds beaks.

A hundred and sixty oarsmen manned the same number of oars on the war galleys. Twenty sailors were on board to raise and lower the sails, handle the anchor, and so on. At least sixty soldiers, including gunners, were also on board. This was a small force compared to the number of soldiers typically manning the warships of other countries, but Venetian oarsmen, unlike those of other, particularly Islamic, countries, were free citizens rather than chained slaves. Thus oarsmen could serve as combatants if the need arose and manpower shortages were unlikely. Cannons were installed only on the ship's bow.

The second type of ship was one degree larger than the thin *galera sottile*. With three masts and over two hundred oarsmen, these ships were twice as tall as the war galleys and had bridges positioned on both the bow and the stern. The roof of the stern bridge on these ships was solidly built; these bridges were inhabitable. Yet, even on these larger ships, cannons could only be found on the bow.

These large galleys moved more sluggishly than the

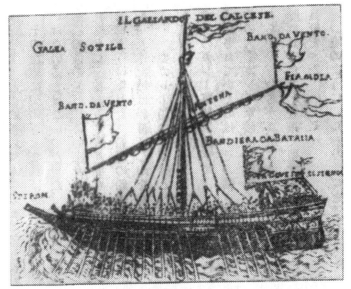

Galley

Galleass

galera sottile and were used mainly as merchant ships; when used in combat they generally served as flagships. The *galera sottile*, on the other hand, were agile and therefore used for the actual fighting. As flagships, the larger galleys were painted entirely crimson rather than the deep brown of the other galleys. This color, which covered even the oars, was commonly called *Rosa Veneziano* and was the same crimson as the Venetian flag upon which San Marco's lion was sewn in gold thread.

Flora's son, who was following Barbarigo around the shipyard as usual, noticed two of the flagships being completed in the dock in front of him. He turned to Barbarigo and asked who would sail on those ships. Barbarigo looked down at the boy by his side, smiled, and answered that no one had yet decided. He didn't imagine then that it would be himself.

There was yet another variety of ship in the yard, one which never failed to draw attention. This was the galleass, which was also known affectionately by the playful nickname "The Bastard." Combining characteristics from both sailing ships and galleys, these ships, a type yet to be seen in other countries, were the latest weapons dreamt up by the late-sixteenth-century Venetian navy.

At forty meters long, they seemed small compared to the flagships. Yet they were close to ten meters wide and could function as sailing ships since they rose ten meters high from the surface of the sea.

Sailing ships primarily used triangular sails, but the

galleasses were also equipped with square sails. While most ships had three main masts, the galleasses had a fourth on the stern. As a hybrid sailing ship and galley, oars were naturally part of the design to ensure free movement regardless of whether or not winds were favorable. Unlike those on war galleys, however, oarsmen on these ships were stationed directly below, rather than atop, the deck. Galleasses fired on the enemy from a distance; they didn't engage in close-quarter combat like the *galera sottile* warships, thus obviating the need for oarsmen to double as soldiers. Placing oarsmen below deck also protected them from enemy fire.

The bulkier galleasses generated more water and wind resistance than the low-lying *galera sottile* and thus maneuvered less easily. They were conceived, however, as floating batteries. Artillery positioned on the bridge used the entirety of the ship's circular bow, which was divided into three levels to allow ten cannons to fire across a 270-degree range. The left and right flanks were both equipped with four cannons, and ten to twelve small cannons were attached to the stern bridge: calling the ship a "battery" is thus no exaggeration. Including muskets, these ships were theoretically capable of firing sixty rounds simultaneously.

The number of sailors on board had to increase accordingly: each galleass required four to five hundred men. Venice had a limited population and it was out of the question for it to fight by using the kinds of "human waves" that the Ottoman Empire was able to muster.

Mobilizing cannons at sea was the most economical and effective use of its limited resources.

That said, Venice couldn't fight naval battles with galleasses alone. The Turks often attacked using small galleys, which rendered the hulking vessels' lack of mobility a major drawback. Venice's strategy was thus to use both galleasses and *galera sottile*. They couldn't rely too much on sails when fighting on the Mediterranean, where winds shifted rapidly.

By early 1570, Venice's shipyard was launching one war galley per day. It continued at this pace over several months and produced a hundred and fifty war galleys, twelve galleasses, and over thirty large sailboats. Although the sailing ships played no direct role in battle, they ferried food and ammunition. In the late sixteenth century, only Venice could build ships in such numbers.

But victory in war is not determined by technical prowess alone. This was particularly true in the sixteenth century, which saw the rise of large nations possessing far more territory than a mere city-state like Venice. And Venice's opponent in this case was the Ottoman Empire, which controlled more territory than any other state at the time.

A Greek man arrived in Venice in mid-February 1570 bearing a message from the Turkish sultan. He was welcomed as a guest at the home of the French ambassador to Venice.

As the Turks did not have a diplomatic corps, they

frequently entrusted even weighty matters to their Greek subjects, who were by necessity multilingual. Without diplomats, there was no need for permanent embassies. In the past, envoys from Turkey had often used ordinary hotels during their stays in Venice, but Turkey and France had joined in an alliance in recent years. That year's Ottoman envoy from Greece therefore stayed as a guest of the French Embassy.

On February 27th, the Greek envoy read the sultan's message in the senate chamber in the Palazzo Ducale and requested an answer. The message, aggressive in tone from beginning to end, demanded the "return" of Cyprus. Not surprisingly, the mood in the chamber grew quite tense. The senate voted 220 to 199 to reject the Ottoman Empire's demand.

The thirty years of peace with Turkey that had begun in 1540 had come to an end.

The mood of impending war, more than anywhere else, totally transformed the state shipyard. Temporary workers and women were mobilized. The sounds of hammers filled the air and new sails were woven at a feverish rate. More and more sailors filled the shipyard while shipwrights were given their respective billets. Barbarigo decided it was best to stop taking the boy with him to the frenzied shipyard. Though bitterly disappointed, the boy understood. Barbarigo had no intention, though, of giving up meeting the boy's mother.

Barbarigo suddenly learned at the end of February

that he had been relieved of his position. He was secretly summoned to the Council of Ten's chambers, where he learn about the new assignment that awaited him.

While the Council of Ten may have had a rather plain and simple name, their organization held immense power. The group in fact consisted of seventeen members: ten councilors, the doge, and six of his deputies.

The doge served for life, but the other sixteen members, while inaugurated at different times during the year, only had one-year appointments. All sixteen of them were chosen from among the senate. Thus, each age group was well represented in the Republic of Venice's government: most of the doges were elderly, the six deputies tended to be in their fifties or sixties, and it was not rare for the other ten councilmen to be in their thirties or forties.

In cases that required secrecy and speed, the Council of Ten was permitted to act at its own discretion, without the necessity for debate in the senate or the assembly. The Council was also the clearinghouse for the information gathered by the republic's espionage organs. Even the fact of being given an assignment by the Council of Ten had to be shrouded in secrecy. In most cases, the name of the individual appointed never surfaced, and Barbarigo's appointment was no different. Upon his request, he was given a three-day postponement for his departure.

The Aegean Sea – Spring 1570

I do not know the secret mission with which Agostino Barbarigo was charged. If one scoured all materials relating to the Council of Ten that remain in Venice's archives, I suspect one could find the answer. I'm afraid, however, that I neglected to do so, and studied only the materials deemed most relevant to the Battle of Lepanto. These records contain no mention of the substance of Barbarigo's secret orders. We can, however, trace the record of his actions. If we combine that knowledge with information from other historical sources, a general outline emerges.

In February 1570, the Venetian government named Sebastiano Veniero as Corfu's *Provveditore*. This official title was unique to the Venetian Republic, and in this case it denoted the military's highest commander, in the same way that "governor" denoted the highest civilian official. Since Corfu was Venice's most important outpost, the selection of Corfu's *Provveditore* was as important as the selection of an ambassador to a major power.

The official title *Provveditore* was also given to Barbarigo when he left Venice under secret orders, but in this case the term is best understood, in line with its etymology, as "inspector" or "investigator." Now that war was inevitable, Barbarigo was responsible for inspecting the preparations at Venice's foreign outposts. He was unofficially selected rather than publicly appointed to the task in order not to provoke the Turks. Under the simple title of inspector, Barbarigo boarded the fast ship that had been prepared to carry Veniero, the *Provveditore* of Corfu, to his own post. This arrangement had also been decided by the Council of Ten.

This was not Barbarigo's first encounter with Sebastiano Veniero. Both had attended a conference to resolve a border dispute between the Venetian Republic and the Austrian Habsburg monarchy six years earlier. Compared to Veniero, who had been the chief delegate, Barbarigo's role had been minor. At that time, Barbarigo had witnessed Veniero's infamous temper. Although approaching seventy-four, Veniero had lost none of his tenacity; his mere appointment as the highest official responsible for protecting Corfu indicated Venice's decision to stand firm against Turkey.

Barbarigo left Veniero on Corfu in March and continued in a different galley to Crete. He intended to carefully inspect the outposts lined up like a rosary along Crete's northern coast. Starting from the west, these included Canea, Suda, Retimo, the capital city Candia, and finally Spinalonga, famous as an impregnable fortress built in the middle of the sea. Turkey at this time gave no indication that it planned to attack Crete, but its policies were decided at the whim of the sultan. Considering Crete's importance, defense preparations could not be neglected.

In a speech that Veniero gave to the senate, he defined the value Venetians placed on their foreign outposts: "Corfu is our gateway to the sea. Zante is a harbor open to all ships sailing the Eastern Mediterranean. Cyprus produces salt, a vital Venetian export, as well as the important exports of wine and cotton. Additionally, it functions as Venice's border. Crete is our most important outpost in the Eastern Mediterranean. Its value is incomparable."

In Crete, Barbarigo met his old acquaintance Antonio da Canale.

The Canales boasted as long an aristocratic lineage as the Barbarigos, but Antonio showed absolutely no sign of his noble heritage. Barbarigo's appearance and manner imparted a feeling of first-class elegance, but Canale, the same age as Barbarigo, was a large, beefy man who looked more at home mingling with the ship hands. Canale's personality, however, was that of a typical sixteenth-century Venetian aristocrat: imbued with a sense of duty.

Although a commander, Canale was unique in not wearing armor into battle. He claimed that being covered from head to foot in steel armor, though safer, constricted his movement. In battle he usually wore a specially made suit of white quilted fabric stuffed with cotton. It had a hood and hung to his feet, resembling a modern ski suit. He looked like a giant polar bear amidst the sailors, who wore predominantly dark clothing, and was quite conspicuous on the front lines. Turkish soldiers feared him, calling him "the White Bear of Mongol." At the end of a battle, this striking outfit would be stained dark red with the blood sprayed from his enemies.

Barbarigo headed for Cyprus on a galley provided by Canale.

The galley was accompanied by two escort ships since they would enter enemy waters once they passed Crete. Cyprus itself was an outpost floating in the middle of enemy territory. Between Crete and Cyprus lay the Isle of Rhodes, Turkish territory since 1522. Moreover, Turkish lands on the southern rim of Asia Minor were only a single night's journey from Cyprus, which was just off the mainland coast.

Blessed with favorable westerly winds, the ship headed east and fortunately avoided meeting any enemy ships. Though the winds meant they didn't need assistance from their oarsmen, a galley moving at top speed powered by full sails rolls ceaselessly from side to side. It was not easy to sleep in the cabins.

Barbarigo, who thought he had been asleep for a while, awoke in pain as he was thrust into the side of the hard, wooden bed. His blanket was now wrapped around his lower body. As he unwound himself, the soft sensation against his hands suddenly reminded him of Flora. He recalled the evening he had learned that there was a fifteen-year age difference between himself and her. He also learned that they had nearly crossed paths at various times in the past.

At twenty he had gone to Florence, accompanying his father who had been dispatched there as ambassador.

Five-year-old Flora lived at that time on the very same street where Barbarigo and his father had stayed. They nearly met again fifteen years later when Barbarigo was thirty-five and visiting Madrid as part of the Venetian delegation to Philip II's coronation. Flora just happened to be in Madrid at that time; her father was traveling on business and had brought his beloved only daughter along. Soon after returning from this trip, Flora's father, who didn't want to part with his daughter and had repeatedly refused requests for her hand, finally agreed to marry her off to a Venetian noble.

Sighing deeply in Barbarigo's arms, Flora had asked why the Lord had not allowed them to meet until now.

"He must have been waiting until we both needed each other," Barbarigo replied.

"If that were the case," she muttered with displeasure, "he would have let us meet in Madrid when we could have gotten married." He smiled without a word and gently caressed her hair.

Whenever he thought of Flora, everything around him came to be filled with thoughts of her. When the spray of the sea entered his mouth, he recalled the night that he had kissed away the tears streaming down the cheeks of her smiling face. "I love you," she'd said to him that night. Every time she whispered those words with that faraway look in her eyes after lovemaking, his love for her grew.

While the assignment awaiting Barbarigo after his

arrival in Cyprus was not difficult, it depressed him. The conditions in Cyprus had not at all improved from the situation he had reported six months earlier, at the time of his return home. The Venetian government had taken no drastic measures to improve things.

Cyprus is the third largest island in the Mediterranean after Sicily and Sardinia. Although Crete is often thought of as being larger, Cyprus's inland areas are extensive. For a state like the Republic of Venice, whose goal was to maintain its colonies rather than extend its territory, Cyprus's major drawback was that it could not be adequately defended.

Furthermore, the island's capital Nicosia was an inland town in the middle of a plain, clearly vulnerable to the mass siege tactics employed by the Turkish army. The various ports where relief supplies were received from the Venetian homeland were along the coast, far removed from Nicosia. Cyprus's largest and strongest fortress was in Famagusta, a port fifty kilometers from the capital. All that lay between the capital city and the island's main harbor was an unbroken expanse of cotton fields.

Less than five thousand troops were stationed in Cyprus. This was because Venice and Turkey had not been at war for over thirty years, and also because Venice lacked manpower—although this was nothing new. That said, a defense force of this size had been sufficient in the past. Until the middle of the fifteenth century, a small force made up of superior soldiers could prove highly effective.

Times had changed, however. In 1570, the enemy was Turkey, whose strategy was to attack in great numbers. Even to capture the tiny Isle of Rhodes, Turkey had sent a hundred thousand soldiers. Cyprus, which was much larger and easier to supply with provisions, would surely be attacked by an even larger force despite its significant distance from Constantinople.

Cyprus's residents were Greek Orthodox and knew that the Turks guaranteed religious freedom throughout their territories, including in Constantinople. Furthermore, few Cypriots understood that Venice could better develop the island's potential and allow it to prosper economically. Venice could not count on Cypriots to help with the defense.

It was nearly the middle of April when Agostino Barbarigo returned to Venice, which was consumed with the impending war. The doge, dressed in dignified formal attire, had led a mass in the Church of San Marco on March 7th, praying for victory against the Turks. That had been Venice's formal declaration of war. The Venetian government had also dispatched an official envoy to Pope Pius V in Rome to explain the need for a united front against the Turks. In response, the Pope had sent an official envoy to the Spanish King Philip II requesting his participation. Venice, meanwhile, was immersed in preparations for war.

A fleet of sixty war galleys had left the docks of San

Marco on March 30th with the goal of aiding Cyprus. Newly installed *Capitano Generale del Mare* Girolamo Zanne commanded the fleet. This, more than anything, was Venice's declaration that it was ready to commence battle. Barbarigo had passed this fleet as his ship moved northward through the Adriatic Sea on the way home to Venice. The fleet then set anchor in Zara, Venice's largest outpost in Dalmatia.

Zanne's promotion to *Capitano Generale del Mare* put the following commanders under his authority: Sebastiano Veniero in Corfu, Marco Quirini and Antonio da Canale in Crete, and Marcantonio Bragadino in Cyprus.

Upon his return, Barbarigo spent several days reporting to the Council of Ten and then returned to his previous assignment at the shipyard. Flora, whose name and presence were both evocative of spring flowers, welcomed him home with radiant delight.

Spring came to Constantinople later than it did to Venice. Ambassador Barbaro had received secret orders from the Council of Ten a month earlier. Under the weight of his added responsibilities, he felt as if the northern winds sweeping across the Bosphorus Strait were cutting into him more deeply than usual.

The Council of Ten, Venice's declaration of war notwithstanding, had ordered Barbaro to explore all possible means of preserving peace with Turkey. This secret order was written barely a day after the Venetian senate had emphatically rejected Turkey's demands. The Venetian Republic's usual approach was always to prepare for war while negotiating for peace, so the Council of Ten's actions were hardly a surprise. That didn't make Barbaro's job any easier, however.

If his desire for peace appeared too ardent, the Turks would take it as a sign of weakness. Nonetheless, he had to keep making overtures while avoiding anything the Turks could interpret as vulnerability, which meant maintaining a firm political stance. Unfortunately, the only man who would listen to reason, the Grand Vizier Sokullu, had clearly fallen into the minority. At the same time, he hadn't actually been replaced as grand vizier, so Barbaro had no choice but to negotiate with him.

Under these circumstances, he had to conduct the negotiations in secret. Barbaro called upon a contact he had earlier cultivated with just such an eventuality in mind, a Jewish doctor name Ashkenazi. He was the physician to the grand vizier's wife, and at some point had become Barbaro's physician as well. Barbaro sent for him almost daily, feigning diarrhea.

Rome – Spring 1570

Besides Marcantonio Barbaro, there was another Venetian diplomat whose claims to be suffering from diarrhea would not have been doubted by anyone. Giovanni Solanzo belonged to one of Venice's best-known families. Like Barbarigo, Barbaro, Canale, and Veniero, Solanzo's family line stretched back over four hundred years. These names required no introduction, not only in Venice, but throughout the royal courts of Europe as well.

The Solanzos had produced countless dignitaries. One of these, Francisco Solanzo, said the following in the early sixteenth century: "A great power can do as it pleases, in times of war as well as in times of peace. We must acknowledge that our Venetian Republic is no longer in such a position."

Giovanni was sent as an envoy extraordinaire and ambassador plenipotentiary to Rome precisely because of the truth of the words quoted above. While the Venetian Republic did possess the ability to launch a galley per day, from the sixteenth century on it had become unable to resist the Turks alone.

Venice's government was uncomfortable relying on its regular ambassador in Rome for such a crucial mission, which was why it went so far as to send a special envoy. The Venetian government had also adroitly avoided informing Solanzo of the secret orders given to Ambassador Barbaro in Constantinople to search for a means to achieve peace. Solanzo, however, was not alone in his ignorance.

It is uncertain how old Giovanni Solanzo was at that time. Based upon his previous and subsequent positions within the government, however, he was probably in his fifties. He applied all of his experience and skills in trying to persuade the Pope to support Venice in war.

Pope Pius V was sixty-six years old and had been elected four years earlier, in 1566.

There had been no chance for Pope Pius V's ascension to be welcomed with cheers and applause. Despite the passage of four years, people continued to view him with fear and suspicion.

Prior to his election as Pope, he had served for thirty years as an inquisitor, and for close to the final ten years he had been the Grand Inquisitor. In one particular case, a bookstore owner was tried, convicted, and dealt a cruel prison sentence for selling a book banned by the Roman Catholic Church. A cardinal at the time, Pius had been the one to find the volume among a raft of other books.

He also publicly criticized Elizabeth I for arresting Mary, Queen of Scots and did not conceal his support for Catherine de Medici during the French Wars of Religion. Not surprisingly, Pius V also despised both the German Protestant monarchs and the Dutch merchant class and didn't hesitate to express this publicly.

He believed that rehabilitating the eternal Catholic

Church, which the Protestant Reformation had put on the defensive, required drastic measures. Only a few years had passed since the conclusion of the Council of Trent where plans to reconstruct the Catholic Church had been debated. The world was in the midst of the Catholic Counter-Reformation spearheaded by the Jesuits, and Pius V, who belonged to the Dominican order, was in all respects a man of the Counter-Reformation.

Many people—particularly the Italians, who traditionally held reason in high regard—feared and distrusted Pius V. They worried that the Vatican might turn into an inquisition tribunal. So far, however, the Pope had been kept busy enough criticizing monarchs for insufficient fidelity to the Church. In Italy, where tolerance still reigned, issues were resolved without such inhumane atrocities as burnings at the stake. Such cruel torture was typical during the Inquisition and had wreaked havoc in other European countries.

There was probably no one less sympathetic to the Venetian Republic, the most tolerant polity in Europe at the time in terms of freedom of religion and speech, than Pius V. The republic needed Christian allies, however. Pius V had pledged to forego meat and eat only eggs until all infidels and heresy had been eradicated.

Venice's plan to convince the fanatical Pius V was far from simple.

Venetian officials were aware of his deep hatred for Venice, which had become powerful through its trade with the infidels. The argument that Venice's commercial outposts in the Orient were imperiled would do little to persuade this Pope. There was the possibility of approaching the King of Spain to win the Pope over, but the Spanish king didn't exactly welcome Venetian power in the Mediterranean. It was likely that he would be more pleased than saddened to see Cyprus taken by the Turks.

Venice's plan, therefore, was to appeal to the egg-eating Pope's crusader mentality. It was absolutely necessary, however, to make the participating monarchs, and even the Pope himself, believe that the idea had originated with Pius V. As part of the ploy, neither the special envoy Solanzo nor the Venetian Council of Ten openly displayed their happiness when Pope Pius V called for the formation of a crusade. At times they even pretended to defy his will. The anti-Muslim crusade had to appear to be the Pope's own initiative or it would have no effect.

Pope Pius V fell for it completely. He became so ardent about the cause that one had to wonder where in that tall, thin body he had been hiding all that passion. Rome sent envoys one after another to meet with Philip II of Spain, who hedged his words and attempted not to give a clear answer. If the Spanish monarch showed even a hint of support for the crusade, Pius V would take it as an opportunity to force the king to commit.

The Venetian Republic frequently angered the Pope. But the angrier he became, the more he seemed to burn with zeal to form an allied fleet against the Turks.

Venice, though, was in a hurry, and Cyprus's precarious position caused the Venetians to become careless. They had devoted so much attention to forming an allied fleet quickly that they hadn't allotted enough time for the proper organization of their own fleet.

Anyone who knew anything about warfare, to say nothing of naval warfare, could see that the allied fleet of 1570 was a hastily assembled hodgepodge. But anyone could also see that time was of the essence.

The Aegean Sea – Summer 1570

It seems the thirty years of peace with the Ottoman Empire had in fact dulled the Venetian government's ability to respond. It was even difficult to convince people that the peace was over. To make matters worse, the replacement of the doge, the central figure in the Venetian Republic's government, also occurred at this time.

The doge served for life. There could be no replacement until he died. Even if the new doge were selected as quickly as possible, Venice would effectively be without a cabinet from the time of the doge's first signs of illness until his death, as well as through the selection period for the replacement. The new doge, Mochenigo, was an anti-Turkish hardliner who took action quickly after assuming office, but the Turks were still able to take advantage of the preceding transitional period.

The primary reason that the 1570 allied fleet was aborted was because it set out at a time when Spain and Venice, its main constituent members, couldn't come to an agreement on anything.

Spain's King Philip II was not a fanatic like Pope Pius V. He realized full well that the allied fleet had been formed to defend Cyprus from the Turks. That said, he was the "Catholic King"—a title that had attached to the Spanish kings for generations—and it would be unwise for the Catholic King to ignore entreaties from the Pope. He thus acceded to the Pope's request, but secretly ordered Gian Andrea Doria, the Genoese he had put in command of Spain's fleet, to engage in no battle that would benefit Venice.

There was no way for them to confirm it, but the Venetians suspected as much. They adamantly opposed Spain's recommendation of Captain Doria as supreme commander of the combined fleet. Although his distinguished uncle Andrea Doria, the mercenary captain nicknamed the "Mediterranean Shark," had already passed away, the Doria family was still famous as naval mercenaries who hired out both ships and sailors.

During Andrea Doria's time, the Doria family first worked for the Pope, then for the French king, and then, in a move considered scandalous at the time, for France's mortal enemy, the Spanish crown. The Doria family was still working for the Spanish king during the time of Gian Andrea, who was Andrea's nephew.

Mercenary captains work for money—that's the nature of the beast. So of course Venice, which suspected the Spanish king's true intentions, was hesitant to entrust its own fleet to such a man. Although they both spoke Italian, Venice and Genoa were polar opposites. Venice may have hired mercenaries for its army, but it only manned its navy with citizens. Furthermore, Venice was providing half the allied fleet and thus lobbied for a Venetian naval officer to be supreme commander. The Spanish king found this unacceptable.

The Pope proposed a compromise, suggesting that the admiral commanding the papal navy, Marcantonio

Colonna, serve as supreme commander of the allied fleet. Neither Venice nor Spain approved. Anyone could see that it was not safe to entrust the combined fleet to Colonna, a man with no naval combat experience whatsoever. With no resolution to the discord among the Christians in sight, the situation grew dire.

In July, three hundred Turkish galleys, fully loaded with a hundred thousand troops, landed on the southern coast of Cyprus. It appeared that they were saving the northern coast of the island, heavily fortified with Venetian troops, for later. The southern coast consisted of only a few harbors used by merchant ships and an endless series of Venetian-operated salt fields. The Turks landed with ease.

The Turkish army then moved north and surrounded Cyprus's capital, Nicosia. Although Venice had sent some additional forces, there were barely three thousand troops in Nicosia. Even after the Venetian government knew for sure that there was a crisis, it sent only four thousand soldiers to defend all of Cyprus.

When the Christian powers received news that Turkish forces had landed on Cyprus, they agreed to make Colonna the temporary supreme commander and ordered their respective fleets to assemble in Crete's Suda Bay.

For Venice, 1570 was a year of setbacks.

They had dispatched a sixty-galley fleet to defend Cyprus at the end of March, one month after they had decided to stand firm against the declaration of war received from Turkey. Girolamo Zanne was the *Capitano Generale del Mare*, which wounded up docking at the harbor town of Zara in mid-April and remained anchored there for two months.

A violent epidemic had raged among the fleet's crew on their way to Cyprus, forcing them to stop barely one-third of the way south into the Adriatic Sea. Shortly after leaving Venice, the crew began collapsing one man after another. When the epidemic subsided two months later, the fleet left Zara and headed toward Corfu, its next scheduled port of call. From there, Zanne sent home a report dated July 5th, five days after the Turkish army had landed on Cyprus.

Venice sent orders to the fleet in Corfu to head for the assembly point in Crete in order to join the allied armada. The papal and Spanish fleets were scheduled to meet in the southern Italian harbor of Otoranto and then proceed to Crete. Yet the Spanish fleet, supposedly under Doria's command, did not arrive. The nearly non-existent papal fleet, consisting only of a few galleys brought along by Colonna, waited in vain in Otoranto. Doria was in Messina, only a few days' journey away, but he hadn't received orders yet from Philip II to ship out.

On August 4th, the 130-galley Venetian fleet, weakened by illness but now including ships from Corfu and Crete, already awaited at the Cretan naval port of Suda. They were anxious to reach Cyprus, where everyone believed a fierce battle was already underway. Yet neither

Colonna nor Doria had shown. The midsummer heat was particularly punishing on the Venetian soldiers who were already weakened by the epidemic. The Venetian commanders waited impatiently; they feared a new outbreak.

Doria finally arrived in Otoranto on August 19th. The anxious Colonna pushed him to set sail for Crete. It wasn't until August 31st that the Spanish-Papal fleet finally reached Suda. The ships accompanying Doria, however, hardly deserved the name "Spanish Fleet," for they were only the mercenary captain's own ships, sailors, and soldiers. There was no chance that this allied fleet, finally assembled, could lift anchor immediately and head east to rush to the aid of Cyprus.

A war council was held on Colonna's ship. Doria was clearly trying to stall, and no decisions were made. He first complained that there were too few soldiers on the Venetian ships. In addition to sailors and oarsmen, war galleys carried soldiers, perhaps best called marines, to act as combatants. Due to the epidemic that had devastated that year's Venetian fleet, however, some ships that usually carried sixty soldiers were only carrying twenty.

The Venetians countered Doria's complaint by pointing out that the oarsmen on Venetian ships were free citizens and could thus assume the role of combatant. Nonetheless, twenty was still a small number. The Venetians tried desperately to reinforce their manpower by recruiting locals from Crete. But naval warfare was Doria's profession, and each of his ships carried a hundred soldiers; the difference in numbers between the two was clear.

The Venetian commanders nonetheless refused to be talked down. Venice was the one providing a hundred and thirty galleys and twelve galleasses. Every time Doria appeared on the verge of backing down, though, he would come up with a new complaint. Now he argued that it was too late in the year to depart for battle. It was not yet the middle of September.

Only a resolute decision from the supreme commander could have ended the stalemate. The supreme commander, however, was Colonna. His calm personality made him suitable as an intermediary, but he simply did not have the temperament to issue orders. It was furthermore impossible to expect firm authority from a supreme commander who hardly had any forces of his own to mobilize.

Colonna did actually want to ship out. Although his manner of persuasion wasted a number of days, he did in the end convince Doria to start sailing eastward.

On September 18th, the allied fleet of the year 1570 set out from Crete. It was composed of 180 war galleys, 12 galleasses, and 30 transport ships. By this time, however, Nicosia had already fallen under the assault of 100,000 soldiers and 60 cannons.

The allied fleet was halfway to Cyprus when it learned that Nicosia had fallen. The city had been defeated on September 8th, ten days before the fleet left

Suda. The three thousand troops defending the city were virtually annihilated. Every Venetian noble leading the defense had died in battle.

After capturing the capital, the Turkish army moved east to besiege Cyprus's strongest fortress, Famagusta. If Famagusta were captured, all of Cyprus would fall into Turkish hands. The Venetian nobles stationed at Famagusta, under the command of Bragadino, must have fought tooth and nail to defend their fortress. But even here, the defenders numbered a meager five thousand. The fortress, which protected the rear of the harbor, ranked with Corfu and Crete in terms of the solidity of its defenses, but the arrival of relief forces would be necessary if the defenders were to prevail in a battle of five thousand against a hundred thousand. Nonetheless, the leaders of the allied fleet en route to Cyprus yet again failed to reach an agreement.

Doria, representing Spain, argued that continuing was useless and that the fleet should turn back. Venice's admirals, naturally, argued to press on, and were supported by Colonna. During their dispute, however, the weather at sea changed. The fleet was struck by torrential winds and rains. Doria's position grew stronger, while Colonna, unaccustomed to rough weather at sea, grew rattled.

The Venetian Commander in Chief Zanne, noticing the change in the group's dynamic, proposed a compromise. For the time being, they would abandon their course to Cyprus and proceed north through the Aegean

Sea. In other words, he proposed to move the fleet out of the storm to attack either Negroponte or Constantinople. Colonna agreed to this plan, but Doria objected. The storm continued to worsen. The days continued to pass without a decision.

On September 24th, they finally decided to turn the 190-odd warship fleet back to the west. According to a Venetian reconnaissance ship, the Turkish fleet in the seas near Cyprus consisted of only 165 galleys. The Venetian admirals Veniero, Quirini, and Canale persisted in their desire to aid Cyprus. Sebastiano Veniero, Corfu's commander, was directing one flank of the fleet.

The commander in chief of Venice's navy, however, was Girolamo Zanne. Zanne himself had changed his opinion a few times about whether they should aid Cyprus or switch to attacking Constantinople. He finally dispatched Marco Quirini to aid Cyprus with twenty-five hundred soldiers aboard his Cretan fleet. Zanne himself took the remaining ships, withdrawing first to Crete, and then to Corfu.

Quirini's rescue fleet, however, had its path blocked near Cyprus by the fleet of the pirate captain Uluch Ali. The fleet ultimately turned back without setting foot on Cyprus. They had given up on Famagusta.

The main Venetian fleet also encountered continual problems as it retreated to Crete and then Corfu. They ran into such incessant violent winds and rains that, when they finally reached Corfu's harbor, the locals gasped at the damage that had been done to the ships. At least those ships made it back to harbor; a significant number of galleys were missing.

Colonna and Doria led their fleets to Messina, Sicily. After enduring severe storms as well, these fleets reached Messina's harbor in late autumn. Doria's was the only fleet to return to its port of departure without the loss of even one ship, not a surprise since he was a consummate professional of the sea.

Thus the allied fleet of 1570 disbanded without once seeing battle. The Turkish assault on Famagusta relented slightly as winter approached, giving the besieged a brief season of reprieve.

Venice – Spring 1571

Venice's special envoy Solanzo believed that it would be a critical year. The Pope's anti-Turkish allied fleet, called "The Holy League," would continue to exist until its goals had been achieved, but its success depended on the actions of the Spanish king. Only the Pope could bring the Spanish king to the table, and Solanzo believed it was essential that the Pope dispatch a proper allied fleet while Famagusta still held out. He renewed his tenacious campaign to persuade the Pope to do so. And this year, the special envoy would play all his cards.

Solanzo's homeland of Venice had its back to the wall. Girolamo Zanne was relieved of his command and ordered back to Venice, where he would stand judgment for dereliction of duty the previous year. The Corfu *Provveditore*, Sebastiano Veniero, took Zanne's place as *Capitano Generale del Mare*, naval commander in chief.

In addition, a new post was created in the Venetian navy. It was a position immediately below the commander in chief entitled *Provveditore Generale*. In this case, the term may be translated as "vice commander in chief," "deputy commander in chief," or "chief of admiral staff." In essence it was this person's responsibility to stay by the commander in chief's side at all times and take over immediately if anything should happen to him. The senate chose Agostino Barbarigo for this role. This appointment had profound meaning.

Since the position was second only to the *Capitano*

Generale del Mare, it clearly required someone with extensive experience and exceptional ability as a naval commander. As of 1571, the Venetian navy had only two people who met this requirement: Marco Quirini, commander of the Cretan naval outposts, and his deputy, Antonio da Canale. Both were quintessential men of the sea who had likely spent more time on the water than on land. One was five years older than Barbarigo and the other was the same age. But the senate chose these two to serve as *Provveditores*, "staff admirals" in this case next in command after Barbarigo. Barbarigo's appointment to the number-two post would probably not have occurred if the senate hadn't chosen Veniero to be their navy's commander in chief.

Sebastiano Veniero had turned seventy-five that year, but there was nothing about him to give one cause for concern. He was exceptionally tall and lean, and although he lacked the agility of his younger days, he showed no sign of frailty. His receding hair and full beard were pure white, but his pinkish complexion was quite youthful. His sharp eyes glistened with life. He had the physical presence of a true leader.

Veniero had served on Corfu less than a year but had completely won over the hearts of the Venetian sailors working the Aegean Sea. They had given him the respectfully affectionate nickname "Monsieur Bastion," French for "Mr. Fortress," or simply, "The Fortress." Veniero, though, was an extraordinarily short-tempered man. Although his dry anger generally calmed easily, if he truly flew into a rage he was impossible to control.

The Venetian navy's commander in chief had to be not only a military leader, but politically adroit as well. This was particularly important in an allied fleet made up of a number of different countries. Given the previous year's failure, the senate above all wanted a naval commander in chief with firm convictions and the ability to carry them out aggressively. The senators chose Veniero unanimously, but they were concerned about his fiery reputation. That was why they placed someone at his side to keep that fire under control. Barbarigo was selected for this reason, not because his experience or track record was more impressive than those of the other candidates. Yet Barbarigo promised to be more than a mere fire blanket. The senate, the doge's six deputies—who had taken part in the selection—and Doge Mochenigo himself all understood this fully.

Barbarigo departed from the docks of San Marco in January 1571. He set off aboard a Venetian flagship painted entirely in "Venetian Crimson." As second-in-command and the man who would replace the naval commander in chief if the need arose, he was entitled to sail on a flagship.

The ship also flew the Venetian Republic's official flags. The flags had crimson backgrounds featuring San Marco's lion embroidered in gold thread. They had been blessed the previous day at a special Mass at the Church of San Marco. Slightly larger than usual, in battle these banners were flown from the bridge at the rear of the flagships. It was forbidden for vessels within the Venetian fleet to fly the captain's own family crest. While the ships of other states flew a variety of flags bearing the aristocratic family crests of those aboard, only the flag of the republic flew on Venetian ships. In addition to these symbols, the fleet also departed with the command baton that the doge had personally deposited with Barbarigo and which was to be handed to Veniero in Corfu.

A second crimson-colored flagship, intended for Commander in Chief Veniero, departed as well, and fifty additional war galleys and twenty large sailing ships. Barbarigo was entrusted to deliver these, along with the state flags and baton, to the naval commander in chief in Corfu. At that point the Venetian fleet of 1571 would prepare for action.

On the Venetian mainland, a push was underway to recruit new soldiers to address the shortage of manpower. Regardless of whether or not the five-thousand-man goal was met, every recruit was to be sent to Corfu.

Barbarigo arrived at Corfu and completed all of his appointed duties, including meeting with Veniero, who had quickly returned from the seas near Crete. Veniero, pleased to see Barbarigo after nearly a year, jokingly thanked him for being his chaperone. Coming from anyone else this would have seemed sarcastic, but Veniero knew his own flaws perfectly well and didn't mind in the least that someone was on hand to keep them in check.

Zanne, the previous naval commander in chief, was

in Corfu, and Barbarigo issued him formal orders to return to Venice. Veniero supplied him with a galley to take him back to Venice, where he was immediately charged with dereliction of duty, tried, convicted, and thrown into prison. Pallavicini, Zanne's marine captain and perennial yes-man, was also recalled and found guilty of the same offense. These two alone were held responsible for the failure of the 1570 expedition.

This was to be Venice's last-ditch effort to save Cyprus. Whether it would succeed or not would depend in large part on Rome. The men in Corfu who would actually mobilize Venice's sea power, including Quirini and Canale (who had both just arrived from Crete), held serious yet candid debates over the course of many days in their fortress. With Veniero chairing the meetings, courtly stuffiness and solemnity were out of the question; it was like a reunion of battle-hardened field commanders. Yet not a single man among them forgot for a moment exactly what the arrival of spring would mean for Cyprus.

Corfu – Spring 1571

The natives of Corfu were Greek. Since it had been a Venetian colony, and a particularly important one, for some four hundred years, there had been large numbers of Venetian immigrants. Bloodlines were thoroughly mixed by the latter half of the sixteenth century, and there were no clear distinctions of heritage on the basis of having a Greek or Venetian surname. This was sharply different from the situation on Venice's equally important outposts of Cyprus and Crete.

Although those two islands had been colonies of Venice for just as long, their residents felt none of the same allegiance to the republic that residents of Corfu felt. On Crete, perhaps because Venetian colonists had assimilated too much with the local residents—in other words, had become overly familiar—there were at times even rebellions against the home government. On Cyprus, however, where formal control had begun only a hundred years ago, the division between Venetians as rulers and Greeks as subjects was still clear.

Corfu's natural environment also differed from that of Crete and Cyprus. Nature was kind on Corfu: water was plentiful, Cyprus trees crowded around lakes, and the climate was mild. Venetians would feel some regret at the thought of being buried on Cyprus or Crete were they to die abroad but had no such feelings towards Corfu. The island's residents didn't neglect Venetians' graves but rather treated them as they did those of their own countrymen.

On Corfu, Agostino Barbarigo stayed in the home of a leading Corfiot merchant who had just returned from a business visit to Constantinople. In the Venetian Republic, soldiers and merchants frequently shared lodgings in this way. Soldiers sailed on merchant ships in their youth, and a merchant might be put in charge of a warship at any time. Venice's lack of manpower meant there was always a demand for polymaths who could serve in any position, be it as a diplomat, politician, soldier, or merchant.

Merchants were also valuable sources of information. Barbarigo learned detailed information from his host about the situation in Constantinople, which was then boiling over with anti-Venetian sentiment.

Barbarigo had known for the past year that Ambassador Barbaro was under house arrest in the Venetian Embassy in Pera; however, he didn't know all of the details. Probably only the Council of Ten did. All that had been discussed in the senate was that the ambassador's reports had continued uninterrupted in spite of his house arrest.

According to the Corfiot merchant's tale, these reports sometimes fell into Turkish hands. But since Ambassador Barbaro had written his reports in code, they couldn't be deciphered. Turkish officials would come to Barbaro's residence demanding that he decode them. Of course, he obliged. He simply omitted those portions he didn't want the enemy to know, rendering any information the Turks gleaned from the report both harmless and useless.

The merchant laughed as he recalled witnessing one such performance. Barbaro didn't breathe a word about what he was doing. The merchant was amazed at just how convincing the deception was.

It is important to keep in mind that, even in explosive situations, other aspects of people's lives go on as usual. Even though Corfu seemed ready to burst with tension in the spring of 1571, new flowers bloomed with each passing day and one could feel the sense of ease in the very air.

The merchant's house faced a small lake. In another few months a season of refreshing breezes blowing across the lake's surface would arrive. But for now it was still spring, and day by day the emerald hue of the cypress trees reflected in the lake grew more vibrant.

Agostino Barbarigo recalled the morning he left Venice.

The doge, his deputies, and almost all of the senate turned out at the docks of San Marco to send off the flagship. The doge was in a dazzling uniform, with Naval Commander in Chief Veniero's wife to his right and Barbarigo's wife to his left, both in splendid ceremonial gown. Celebratory chimes rang out from the bell tower of the Church of San Marco, while gun salutes echoed from boats along the flagship's path.

The state flag high atop the mast, the crimson flagship caught the wind as its gold thread glittered in the sunlight. Crowds gathered at the docks of San Marco and the Schiavoni embankment to see the ornate procession of war galleys that followed Barbarigo's flagship. Everyone believed that this was the year they would finally confront the Turks in direct combat.

As Barbarigo stood on the deck and exchanged farewells with the people sending him off, he noticed the woman he loved among the crowds filling the docks. Even he was amazed that he had recognized her amidst the crowd, but she, and she alone, seemed to stand out in his field of vision. He held her gaze, firm in the conviction of his love for her. Her son was next to her, shouting and waving like everyone else.

The day Barbarigo was named second-in-command, the date of his departure decided, the boy begged him to take him along. Word had gotten out that Pasqualigo, captain of one of the war galleys accompanying Barbarigo, was bringing along his twelve-year-old brother. But Barbarigo categorically refused the boy's request and told him that eleven was too young. The boy persisted, arguing that a twelve-year-old was going and that he was almost twelve himself. Barbarigo didn't budge. At that age, he said, one year made a big difference. The boy still seemed dissatisfied but didn't press the issue. Though age was a major factor, Barbarigo didn't refuse because of that alone. More importantly, he felt deeply in his heart that the boy should stay with his mother.

Flora didn't cry the evening Barbarigo was given his orders to ship out. She merely said in a hollow voice, "If anything should happen to you, I cannot go on living." She had bravely lived and raised her son on her own. But now, perhaps because the year they had spent together had so accustomed her to his presence, she had lost her former resolve.

He was departing for war and didn't want to patronize her with empty words. In truth, he didn't know what would happen. If he took her son and something were to happen to him, surely she wouldn't be able to go on living. If something happened to himself, on the other hand, she would find a way to go on as long as the boy was with her. Barbarigo wouldn't have wanted to take the boy along even if he were sixteen.

He could say nothing to Flora or her son about when he would return. He himself did not know. Nor did they ask. He did, however, promise to write.

Those letters were the only thing that distressed him while he was in Corfu. Barbarigo had no problem with tasks to which he was accustomed, such as repairing the outpost's fortress, preparing cannons, replenishing gunpowder, and restoring galleys. This was particularly true in Corfu, where he could count on the locals to provide as much assistance as any Venetian. And he was not unaccustomed to writing. One of his responsibilities as second-in-command was to write nearly daily reports to the home government. Yet when it came to writing to the boy and his mother, he had no idea where to begin. Days passed.

Finally, he decided to write to them as if he were composing one of his daily reports: a list of what he had done each day, whom he had met, where he had gone, and so on. Knowing that his letters might be intercepted by the enemy, he of course never included potentially sensitive information. Once he had amassed a decent number of pages, he would send a letter off by regular mail by one of the fast ships that left for Venice every two days. The only hint of tenderness in these businesslike letters was the one line at the very end: "Yours with love, Agostino."

Somehow, these seemingly dry and insipid letters pleased Flora immensely. In response, her letters also became like veritable diary entries. Flora and the boy's life in Venice, one of mutual love and dependence, seemed to come to life right before his eyes.

Although Barbarigo addressed his letters to Flora, the letters she sent in reply always listed the boy as the sender, to conceal their true origin. The pity he felt at seeing this was great indeed.

Constantinople – Spring 1571

The Venetian ambassador Barbaro had lost his freedom exactly one year earlier, in the spring of 1570—May 5th to be exact. A special sixteen-member detachment of Janissaries—the sultan's imperial guards—visited the Venetian embassy in Pera on that day. The detachment commander read aloud an order stating that the ambassador and all embassy staff were considered a danger to the state and would be confined to the embassy.

In truth, Barbaro hadn't expected this. He had assumed that the Turkish government, which didn't recognize diplomatic immunity, would lock the ambassador and embassy staff in the Rumeli Hisari fortress prison along the Bosphorus once war with Venice began. Instead, the Turks merely prohibited them from leaving the embassy. This raised Barbaro's spirits. It was proof that some desire existed in the Turkish court to preserve relations with Venice.

A group of military engineers came one morning and boarded up the embassy's windows. From then on, even at noon, the embassy staff spent their days in candlelight. Still, they hadn't been thrown in prison, and even under these conditions the ambassador continued to send reports to the home country and to contact Grand Vizier Sokullu, the leader of the moderate faction at the Turkish court.

He was able to send reports home because, despite

the boarded windows, there were still people visiting the embassy. It would have been impossible, in fact, to prohibit visitors, most of whom were Venetian merchants still doing business in Constantinople. They typically needed to send business messages to branches back home, in Venice's various commercial outposts, and in major European cities. At that time, Venice was the only country in Western Europe with regular mail service to and from Turkey, and the Venetian post office was located within the Venetian embassy. Not only Venetian merchants, but those of other countries as well, had no choice but to visit the embassy for this reason.

Merchants who came to use the post office could also be used to send confidential messages. It was common knowledge that Venetian citizens abroad, including merchants, were no different from spies. If the ambassador made such a request, nearly everyone would comply. Similarly, none refused to lend his name to confidential messages disguised as commercial correspondence.

Since the Venetian embassy was the only place offering regular mail service with Western Europe, other countries' ambassadors to Constantinople also regularly used Venetian mail. While the system originally developed out of commercial necessity, Venice's mail service provided a high degree of security, confidentiality, and speed, even though all mail had to pass through Venice first.

Furthermore, messages could be relayed through the French ambassador in Venice. At the time France, motivated by its animosity towards Spain, clearly favored doing whatever benefited Venice.

Venice didn't trust foreigners, however, and so didn't take advantage of these offers from the French. By the same token, though the Venetian postal service guaranteed speedy and safe delivery of other countries' diplomatic messages, the Venetians never neglected to read them first.

Though efficient, this postal system didn't completely guarantee safe delivery. This was because it emphasized speed and regularity and couldn't rely solely on sea routes from Constantinople to Venice. Mail was frequently sent across Turkish-controlled land from Constantinople to the town of Cattaro on the Adriatic Sea, and then by fast ship to Venice. As relations between Turkey and Venice worsened, Turkey attempted to intercept Venetian mail. Although Venetian officials tried changing departure dates and disguising messengers, a certain amount of mail still fell into Turkish hands.

The Venetian ambassador therefore began writing his messages in code. The method of writing with a mixture of lemon juice and milk, a technique popular in the Middle Ages, had ended long before. This "ink" disappeared after writing, but reappeared when placed near fire. The problem was that the Turks were already familiar with this technique.

Venetian diplomats used many codes that ranged from the simple to the complex. They also used a number of different codes during any given period of time.

The first method utilized a small, circular decoder chart. The letters of the alphabet were written around its outermost ring. Several languages, including Latin, Greek, and Turkish were then lined up on concentric rings as one moved toward the center of the circle. Using this, a message that appeared to be written in Latin could be decrypted into a message in Italian.

The second method was to prearrange a mutually understood system of letter substitutions, for example "A" would signify "S," "B" would signify "A," and so on.

The third method the Venetians used was to write horizontally from left to right, but to make alternating vertical jumps with each subsequent letter. For example, the word *flotta*, meaning "fleet," would become:

FOT
LTA

The problem with these methods was that they could all quickly be recognized as codes. There was thus a fourth method, one employed rather frequently. Messages in this fourth code looked like musical notation on a standard five-line staff. Each note represented a letter of the alphabet. The recipient would write the corresponding letter under the notes to produce the intended message.

Though this may seem like a rather clever method, sending large amounts of sheet music from the Venetian embassy in Constantinople to Venice would clearly appear strange, and the Turks inevitably paid close attention to anything out of the ordinary. For this reason, messages thus encoded were dispatched through every other means imaginable, such as sending them with merchants going home to Venice, or sending them first to Crete and having them forwarded from there.

In his five years as ambassador to Constantinople, including the three under house arrest, Barbaro sent over four hundred reports to Venice—or at least, that was the number the Venetian government received. Over half were written in code.

The Turks were never able to decipher these codes, which led to the farcical scenario of Turkish officials carrying intercepted letters to the confined Venetian ambassador. Barbaro, in turn, completely altered the import of these messages into whatever it was he thought the Turks wanted to hear.

Barbaro's contact with the Turkish court's moderate faction continued in secret with the aid of his Jewish doctor, Ashkenazi. But at some point Piali Pasha, the influential head of the Turkish hardliners and the sultan's closest adviser, summoned the doctor and demanded to know the true purpose of his frequent visits to the grand vizier's residence. Ashkenazi managed to improvise an explanation, but the episode frightened him. He understood they were in danger and immediately informed the grand vizier and Barbaro that someone had undoubtedly leaked their secret.

Suspicion fell on the interpreter who attended the meetings between Ashkenazi and the grand vizier. Because the doctor's Turkish was not fluent, the grand vizier's translator usually attended their meetings.

It seems these suspicions were warranted. The grand vizier and Barbaro, communicating through Ashkenazi, decided to kill the translator. The Jewish doctor prepared a poison, and the grand vizier administered it. The result was a success. Ambassador Barbaro wrote in one of his usual coded reports to the Venetian Council of Ten, "Five days ago, the doctor completed his task." That was February 19, 1571.

Nonetheless, his labors as his country's chief diplomat to an enemy state were far from over. The Venetians' emissary to their ostensible ally Rome wasn't having an easy time of it, either.

Rome – Spring 1571

The winter of 1570-71 felt horribly long and harsh for Solanzo, who had been sent to Rome as Venice's envoy extraordinaire and ambassador plenipotentiary. He had to form a viable Holy League by spring, no matter what. His hopes rested on the crusader mentality of Pope Pius V, whose energy didn't seem to be flagging at all in spite of his exclusive diet of eggs.

In March, cardinals carrying personal messages from the Pope headed to the courts of various nations, regardless of whether or not the weather in Europe made such journeys practical. Before they even departed, however, Solanzo knew the results would not be favorable. The monarchs had their own political concerns, and they had been alienated by Pius V's reactionary religious statements.

The Holy Roman Emperor Maximilian II, who ruled over Germany, Austria, and Hungary, had entered into a non-aggression pact with Sultan Selim the previous year in an effort to forestall Turkish attacks on his own territory. Needless to say, his reply was not to the Pope's satisfaction.

France was under the reign of Charles IX, but Catherine de Medici was serving as regent. Embroiled in a religious war between Catholics and Huguenots, France did not have the resources to join the alliance; in fact, its animosity towards Spain had led it to form a union with the Turks themselves, making its participation in any anti-Turkish alliance decidedly unlikely.

It was the age of Elizabeth I in England, but the Pope's special envoy wasn't even able to meet with the queen when he arrived in London. The Pope had angered the queen by publicly proclaiming his support for Mary Stuart; an indiscreet remark to the effect that he wanted to wield the dagger that plunged into Elizabeth's heart also didn't help. It would be impossible to expect England to dispatch even a single knight.

The Portuguese king's reply was also negative. Martin Luther's claim that the Turkish people were ten times closer to the truth than the Pope in Rome meant that the Protestant German princes did not care to listen, either. The Maltese Knights of St. John were equal to Pius V in their crusading desire to overthrow Islam, but they had exhausted all of their forces six years earlier in battle with the Turks and were in no condition to take part. They nonetheless sent word that they would contribute three war galleys led by the head of the Knights himself.

Mantova, Ferrera, Savoy, Urbino, Lucca, and Genoa agreed to participate, though on a small scale. But these were minor Italian states, not the great powers that truly ruled Europe. Savoy and Genoa were the only two that could supply even a few war galleys. The others only sent soldiers led by their monarchs' relatives or other noblemen.

The Grand Duchy of Tuscany, of which Florence was the capital, also agreed to participate. The Vatican had no navy worthy of the name, and Tuscany agreed to provide it with one. The Vatican, which was after all the alliance's primary advocate, didn't want to be militarily powerless as it had been during the previous year's botched expedition. The Pope had therefore appealed to Tuscany, which had just begun building ships in hopes of becoming a naval power in its own right. Grand Duke Medici agreed to the Pope's special request, believing it would secure his own rule over Tuscany. The duke promised twelve war galleys as well as soldiers to man them. This marked the birth of the papal fleet of the Grand Duchy of Tuscany.

Under these circumstances, the alliance's two main participants this time would again be Venice and Spain. The Pope's special envoy focused his attention on the court in Madrid, since everything would ultimately come down to Philip II's decision.

Convincing him would not be easy. Throughout March and April, letters and emissaries went back and forth between Rome and Madrid. The Venetians wanted, at all costs, to maintain the appearance that the Pope was the main proponent of the plan, so they refrained from petitioning the king too aggressively. Venice's ambassador to Madrid limited his efforts to convincing the king that Venice was firm in its intent to wage war. This would make it more difficult for the Spanish king to refuse joining.

There were three reasons why Spain didn't care for Venice.

First, the Republic of Venice was the only Italian state standing in the way of Spain's desire to control the entire Italian peninsula. Spain already controlled the area from Naples to Sicily in the south and the land centering on Milan and Genoa in the north. The king had given the grand duke of Tuscany a Spanish wife and had also succeeded in placing the Vatican, which was controlled by Counter-Reformationists, under his influence. The only entity obstructing Spain's goal, and a powerful one at that, was the Venetian Republic.

Second, Venice practiced religious tolerance despite being Catholic. This stood in contrast to Spain, which prided itself on being the epicenter of the fiercely intolerant Counter-Reformation. Venice had a long history of regularly diverging from the Vatican regarding the separation of church and state. It was virtually the only Western European state at the time that sanctioned freedom of religion.

Those unfortunate enough to be caught in the Inquisition's net, if able to escape, could only feel safe upon entering Venetian territory. One could buy and read books the Pope had banned as being unsuitable for good Christians in Venice without fear of being burned at the stake. Luther, Machiavelli, and the erotic poetry of antiquity openly lined Venice's bookstore shelves.

Third, although both Spaniards and Venetians were ethnically Latin, their national characters were extremely different. Without a doubt, Don Quixote could never have been born in Venice. The antagonism between these two countries was both cultural and historical.

Their relationship, however, was complicated by the fact that they could not simply exist as adversaries. The Venetian Republic was no longer able to repel the Turkish threat by itself. By the same token, if Spain wanted to satisfy its territorial ambitions in North Africa, Venetian naval power would be indispensable. In other words, both states needed the help of the other to confront their enemies. Both would have been happy to see the other's power decrease, but each would also be unable to do anything without the other.

In terms of religion, however, the two were completely at odds. From an uninformed observer's point of view, the Pope's attempts to negotiate an alliance between them were doomed to fail. Ultimately, it was the Venetian Republic that needed the formation of the combined fleet more than anyone else. Special Envoy Solanzo had already been instructed by the home government in March to accept a compromise at the last moment.

The scale of the Holy League's combined fleet was set at two hundred warships and fifty thousand soldiers. A fleet any smaller than that would be unable to oppose the Turkish armada. The first issue to address was the relative burden that each of the participating countries would bear. The question of burden sharing was not limited to vessels; galley battles meant hand-to-hand combat, which made soldiers as valuable as ships.

Solanzo was particularly persistent in these negotiations. He knew the allied fleet would be doomed to failure again if Spain only provided Doria's mercenary fleet. No matter what it took, they had to extract a fleet from Spain. This was not a matter of the number of ships or soldiers; what mattered was the significance of the Spanish king's willingness to participate.

The participants' share of the fiscal burden was as follows: Spain, one half; Venice, one third; the Vatican, one sixth. When these ratios are compared to the ratio of warships provided by the participants, it becomes clear that soldiers' pay was weighed heavily. Spain offered 73 ships (15 from Spanish ports, 36 from Spanish-controlled Naples and Sicily, and 22 from Doria's mercenary fleet); the Vatican, 12 ships; the small Italian states, 11 ships; the Knights of St. John, 3 ships; and last but not least, Venice, 110 ships, for a grand total of 209. These numbers were not arbitrarily determined contributions but were simply what each country could provide. Also, these were no more than projected numbers. The actual figures would not be certain until all ships dropping anchor at the assembly port were counted, since shipwrecks en route were a distinct possibility.

Next, the alliance needed to consider its strategic objectives. Venice was adamant on this issue, since it was precisely ambiguity in this regard that had led to the failure of the previous year's fleet. This year, their objectives had to be spelled out in detail.

Venice's motive was to aid Cyprus. Spain wanted to use the allied fleet to attack North Africa. The Pope didn't care where they fought, as long as they were fighting Muslims. Since war between Christians and Muslims had actually broken out on Cyprus, he thought the natural course for the allied fleet was to head in that direction. Spain, believing it had enough leverage to sway the decision, firmly refused to limit the alliance's strategic objectives only to the Eastern Mediterranean. This was not unreasonable and so first the Pope and then Venice had no choice but to acquiesce.

The alliance decided to set out and fight the enemy wherever they were, regardless of whether that meant fighting in the Eastern or Western Mediterranean. They further decided that if Turkey invaded Venetian territory, all other members of the alliance, including Spain, had a duty to come to Venice's aid. Similarly if Turkey invaded Spanish territory, the other allies, including Venice, had a responsibility to offer support. This was a major achievement for Solanzo, who had been struggling to produce a clear statement of intent to aid Cyprus. He probably assumed that Cyprus, currently under Turkish attack, qualified as Venetian territory under the agreement. Assumptions and explicit declarations are two different things, however.

Other items were also agreed upon. The fleet of the Holy League would set out every year, completing its preparations in March and setting sail in April. Of course, they were still in the midst of negotiations in March and April of 1571. Any territory acquired in battle from the Turks would be returned to its prior rulers.

Tunisia, Tripoli, and Algeria, however, would become Spanish territory. It had become impossible for Venice to import wheat from Turkey, so Spain guaranteed that the southern Italian region of Puglia would direct wheat exports to Venice. At the time, southern Italy was Spanish territory.

Ultimately, the greatest obstacle was selecting the fleet's supreme commander.

Venice, as they had the year before, strongly opposed Spain's recommendation of Gian Andrea Doria. Spain, however, opposed Venice's nomination of the Venetian navy's commander in chief, Sebastiano Veniero. Negotiations essentially deadlocked when both Venice and Spain rejected the Vatican's compromise proposal of Marcantonio Colonna.

A resolution came at the beginning of May, when Venice conceded to Spain's second proposal, the Austrian Duke Don Juan. Venice feared that everything would collapse if they resisted any further. Even in Madrid, though, few people knew if Don Juan possessed the ability to direct the combined fleet as supreme commander. Venetian naval commanders in particular, who had never heard of him, wondered, "Who is this Don Juan?"

The man who had suddenly emerged onto the international stage and who was to be known there as "The Austrian Duke Don Juan" had just turned twenty-six that year. He was the half brother of the Spanish King Philip

II, but the two men had not been raised together. Don Juan had been born in the southern German town of Regensburg in 1545 to King Carlos, the prior Spanish king, and a German lady aristocrat. He was raised in secrecy by one of Carlos's retainers until the age of fourteen. King Carlos died when the boy was thirteen, and the following year Philip II, who had succeeded the throne, officially recognized the fourteen-year-old Don Juan as his younger brother.

It was originally planned for Don Juan to enter the priesthood, but as he grew he began to show an interest in military affairs. His older brother decided to put him in charge of Spain's military, perhaps recognizing his potential in that area.

At twenty-three Don Juan participated in the Algerian campaign. The following year he led the expedition to abolish Islam in southern Spain. That was his war record as of 1571. Although he had been victorious in both engagements, they were both land battles. He had no experience fighting at sea. Entrusting a huge fleet of two hundred ships to a young nobleman without naval experience caused Venice's naval leadership great concern. It was Solanzo's job to put these worries to rest.

The king's younger brother was a more prestigious candidate for the job than a mercenary like Captain Doria, though less impressive than the king himself.

The Venetian envoy stated that Don Juan's nobility made him acceptable to Venice as the supreme commander. The truth was that they just wanted to take the untrustworthy Doria out of the running. Since there were concerns about Don Juan's abilities as a naval commander, Solanzo made a counterproposal: Don Juan would be the supreme commander of the allied fleet, but he would consult Veniero and Colonna in all matters; no decisions would be acted upon unless agreed to by all three. Philip II accepted this condition, probably because he imagined that his control of the supreme commander's post through his brother would allow him to do as he wished.

The same condition applied to the lieutenant supreme commander. Since the Pope was the standard-bearer for the alliance, the post was expected to be filled by someone from the papal fleet, making Colonna the obvious choice. He was immediately to assume command if anything should happen to the supreme commander. Given Colonna's performance the previous year, this was hardly reassuring. The stipulation of shared decision-making was intended to relieve some of the anxiety of entrusting such a large fleet to two essential amateurs.

The fleet's assembly point was set in Messina, Sicily. The assembly date could not yet be decided because there were so many different countries contributing resources, and the five thousand soldiers sent directly from Venice still hadn't arrived in Corfu.

The Holy League was officially established in Rome on May 25, 1571 by the signatures of the representatives from the participating states. At a special Mass held in San Pedro's Basilica, the Pope blessed the alliance flag, which was to be flown high atop the mast of the supreme commander's flagship. The alliance had been born after a difficult labor, and it would take several months before a proper upbringing could even begin.

On June 18th, Ambassador Barbaro in Constantinople received top-secret orders from the Council of Ten directing him to end peace negotiations with Turkey. With this, the Republic of Venice finally committed itself to war. According to a coded reply sent by Barbaro, the Turkish fleet had just left the harbor heading south under Ali Pasha's command.

Messina – July 1571

Since the papal navy led by Colonna was a small fleet, it moved into action comparatively smoothly after the establishment of the alliance. On June 15th, Marcantonio Colonna departed Rome after receiving a grand send-off and traveled to the Papal States' main port, Civitavecchia, where the flagship would pick up more passengers. Waiting for the fleet were the Pope's nephew and the Colonna family, but even men of the Orsini family, the sworn enemies of the Colonnas, were there as well. All of the Roman aristocracy were represented, making for a truly majestic spectacle. There were also twenty-five Swiss Guards and a hundred and eighty foot soldiers sent by the Pope from the Roman garrison.

The twelve war galleys provided by the Duke of Tuscany had all arrived in Civitavecchia harbor with an array of Florentine nobles aboard. Most of these aristocrats were wearing the uniforms of Florence's thriving religious order, the Knights of St. Stephen. Colonna gave orders for the remaining Italian ships to gather in Messina as soon as they had completed their preparations. He left Civitavecchia on June 21st with twelve war galleys and headed for Naples, the next port of call.

They entered port at Naples on June 24th. It had been prearranged that Colonna's fleet would wait in Naples for Don Juan to arrive from Spain; they would head to Messina together with the main force of the Spanish fleet. Colonna had therefore brought to Naples the blessed flag of the Holy League, which under normal circumstances Don Juan would have personally received from the Pope's own hands. Don Juan's appointment as supreme commander of the Holy League could not officially begin until he was in possession of the flag.

Don Juan, however, didn't arrive. Spain, which controlled southern Italy from Naples to Sicily, had stationed the king's representative, the viceroy, in Naples. When Colonna questioned the viceroy, he simply responded that he knew nothing about where Don Juan was. Loyal even if not terribly gifted, Colonna had adopted Pius's fervor to form an allied fleet. After three weeks of waiting in Naples, he decided that it would be best for the papal fleet to be in Messina. He decided to leave the alliance flag with the viceroy. The fleet left Naples on July 15th, headed south through the Tyrrhenian Sea, and entered Messina's harbor the evening of July 30th.

The Venetian fleet under Veniero had arrived a week earlier. Messina is on the eastern tip of Sicily facing the Italian peninsula, from which it is separated by a narrow but rapid strait. Although the Venetian fleet had arrived first, it had not been an easy voyage. They had had to make some bitter choices and sacrifices along the way.

Even before the main Turkish fleet left port, Turkish officials had ordered the pirate Uluch Ali to commence all-out guerrilla warfare against the Venetian fleet. Uluch Ali, a native Italian and former Christian, directed twelve high-speed galleys in a concentrated attack on the Venetian ships heading to aid Cyprus. As a pirate, he knew the Mediterranean like the back of his hand and, traveling with small vessels, was able to move extremely quickly. Just when one thought he was near Cyprus, he would appear near the Isle of Rhodes; a few days after pillaging the southern coast of Crete, he would turn up in the waters near Malta.

And he was bold. He even sank three large Venetian sailing ships off the coast of Corfu while the Venetian fleet was moored there on their way to Cyprus. His far-ranging exploits made the journey to Cyprus nearly impossible once the Venetian fleet had passed east of Crete. Meanwhile, Uluch Ali was unable to penetrate the Adriatic Sea because Venice had battle fleets stationed at Corfu, and also Crete.

It would thus have been more practical for the Venetians to remain at Corfu and Crete, but a delayed arrival at Messina would have meant a delayed departure for the combined armada. The Venetian Admiral Sebastiano Veniero had thus been forced to make a painful choice.

He ultimately decided to head for Messina with only the fleet at Corfu. He sent word to the fleet in Crete that they were to leave immediately for Messina once they received orders.

Veniero had to pay a steep price to bring the combined fleet together in this fashion: the waters from Corfu to Crete were essentially left undefended. Venice by this point no longer had the leeway to keep fleets on

Corfu and Crete while sending a separate one to Messina. Veniero took fifty-eight war galleys and three galleasses with him to Messina. He planned for Marco Quirini to arrive with sixty ships from Crete.

It's understandable that Veniero wasn't smiling when Colonna finally arrived after having made him wait a week. The Venetian admiral's anger exploded, however, when he heard that the reason was because Don Juan hadn't shown up.

Marcantonio Colonna, thirty-six years old, looked more like a courtier than a military commander. He was short and thin, and was already balding. His abnormally large eyes left the impression that he had often been sick as a child. Veniero was tall and broad, with white hair swept back. He may not have been screaming in rage, but when he loudly confronted Colonna he looked like an eagle about to swoop down on a dove.

Colonna, however, was an exceptionally loyal servant to Pope Pius V. As a member of the Colonna family, the noblest of Roman houses, he was also known to be on friendly terms with the Spanish royal family. A Venetian admiral was simply in no position to hector a man of his station. Agostino Barbarigo, who was also present, salvaged the situation by changing the subject.

Barbarigo asked Colonna about Doria, who had been directing the Spanish fleet. The amiable Colonna, with audible relief in his voice, enthusiastically addressed this topic. He told Barbarigo that Doria had been traveling from country to country, asking each to contribute what few ships they could spare, and that his arrival at Messina appeared imminent although Colonna didn't know for sure. What Veniero, Colonna, and Barbarigo all did know, but never said, was that everything hinged on Don Juan's arrival.

Don Juan, object of everyone's concern, had already left Madrid on June 6th and was headed towards Barcelona. The Marquis de Santa Cruz was waiting in Barcelona Harbor with the war galleys that were to accompany them. All preparations were complete and they were ready to ship out at any moment. Every couple of days, however, the departure date was pushed back: Philip II had ordered the fleet to take two young German Hapsburg nobles to Genoa. They had been visiting the Spanish Habsburgs and were going to return to Germany but had not yet completed their preparations to leave.

Don Juan waited in the hot Barcelona summer. The nobles finally arrived from Madrid, and they were able to depart on July 20th. Forty-three days had passed since Don Juan's arrival in Barcelona. They arrived in Genoa on July 26th, but they couldn't leave Genoa's harbor right away; they had to attend a farewell banquet being held in honor of the German nobles, which cost them three days. They also had to take aboard six thousand German soldiers, two thousand Italian soldiers, and one thousand Spanish soldiers.

At that time, fleets did not leave port fully prepared

for battle. It was normal for war galleys to leave port with a group of commanders, sailors, and oarsmen aboard, while more soldiers were picked up at ports of call along the way. Soldiers, who were usually mercenaries, assembled in each port of call and waited for their ships, which necessitated frequent stops. This was the case with Spanish fleets, which used slaves as oarsmen.

The Venetian fleet, on the other hand, traditionally hired free citizens even as oarsmen. Venetian vessels had only commanders and the sailing crew aboard when it left home but picked up both soldiers and oarsmen at various ports along the Adriatic. They were fully manned by the time they reached Corfu.

The ships Don Juan brought from Spain needed to be outfitted in Genoa. The group left Genoa for Naples on August 5th. They entered the port at Naples on August 9th, where they spent ten days on, among other things, a ceremony for receiving the Pope's Christian battle flag. Then, on August 23rd, Don Juan's fleet appeared off the coast of Messina.

Messina – August 1571

The long-awaited Don Juan arrived suddenly in Messina's harbor without sending an advance ship. The sun was starting to set behind the mountains on the opposite shore. The strait was quiet in the calm of the evening and the sea was a shining golden expanse.

Neither Colonna nor Veniero had time to line up their fleets in greeting. Still, cannon fire rang out in welcome from shore, and small boats carrying Venetian and Vatican dignitaries were launched. It would be their first glance at the new supreme commander; they excitedly crowded along their boats' bows and watched the grand flagship approach. Surely the young man standing at the prow was Don Juan. He was tall and slender, and even with the evening sun at his back one could tell that he had an extremely pale complexion. Don Juan's eyes were pure blue, his hair a dazzling gold. His posture suggested a man of elegant bearing.

He saw Colonna's and Veniero's ships lined up in welcome on either side and now smiled. His smile had the ease and amiability available only to those with a perfectly unaffected sense of their own noble origins.

Cheers arose simultaneously from the ships crowding the harbor and the people waiting on shore. The calls of "Don Juan!" and "Don Giovanni!" in both Spanish and Italian filled the narrow strait. The young noble continued to respond with a natural smile and a raised hand. This kind of thing puzzled the Venetians, who prided themselves on their republican system. There was no one in the Republic of Venice whose mere appearance could excite this kind of emotion.

Veniero and Barbarigo felt both a sense of relief and a grudging recognition of Don Juan's value. The only remaining question was whether or not he could carry out his essential duties as supreme commander. At the very least, though, the young noble's arrival had inspired hope and expectation among the sailors and soldiers.

On the assumption that the long journey had left the supreme commander fatigued, there was no welcome banquet that evening. The commanders also delayed assembling for the war council until the following day.

Only Colonna, in his capacity as lieutenant supreme commander, met with Don Juan. While the content of their hour-long discussion is unknown, Colonna later sent a letter to the Pope stating that the meeting was to make sure that Don Juan understood that all decisions were contingent upon the agreement of all three admirals.

A courtier by nature, Colonna was an astute observer and had most likely noticed the constant presence of Lord Requeséns by Don Juan's side. In fact, Philip II had ordered the Spaniard Requeséns to accompany Don Juan as his counsel, or more precisely, his chaperon. Colonna had wanted to meet Don Juan alone, without this other man present.

The first war council was held the following day, the 24th, aboard the supreme commander's flagship. Don Juan attended as chair, with Veniero and Barbarigo representing Venice. From the Vatican were Marcantonio Colonna and troop commander Prospero Colonna. There were also representatives from Savoy, Genoa, and Malta, which had supplied ships and men. Soldiers had been provided by Florence, Lucca, Ferrara, and Mantova, and representatives from these states attended as well.

Lord Requeséns stood motionless behind Don Juan. Requeséns had received secret orders from the Spanish king to postpone the allied fleet's departure as long as possible. If it became impossible to delay any longer, he had been instructed to try to direct the fleet towards North Africa.

The first war council was spent confirming the number of ships and sailors. The Venetians, though, quickly noticed the Spaniards' stalling tactics.

"Those pasty-faced schemers from Madrid are a perfect match for their king!" Veniero spat out to Barbarigo as they were riding on a skiff back to their ship.

At the second war council the leadership decided to dispatch a reconnaissance ship. No one denied the need to know more about enemy movements, but Lord Requeséns proposed the use of a Spanish ship for this assignment. Veniero flatly refused, on the grounds that Venetians knew the Eastern Mediterranean best. The Spaniards, for their part, wouldn't consent to sending only a Venetian ship. Colonna proposed a compromise of sending a Spaniard as captain and a Venetian as first mate. This was deemed acceptable.

With circumstances such as these, the daily war councils inevitably fell further and further behind schedule. There were also the language barrier.

The Spaniards only spoke Spanish so Veniero needed a translator. Although Colonna could have served in this capacity, Veniero considered the Roman noble an ally of Spain and didn't trust his translations. The conversation slowed to a crawl as Barbarigo, whose Spanish was less than perfect, did the translating. Which is not to say that incomprehension would have reigned had no translator been present: the Spaniards and the Italians understood a bit of one another's languages. Obscenities, in particular, were immediately understood.

Quirini arrived in Messina from Crete on September 2nd with the second Venetian fleet of sixty ships. Doria and his twenty-two ships, coming from Genoa, also sailed into the port that evening. The southern Italian fleet led by the Marquis de Santa Cruz arrived on the following day.

With that, the armada was complete. Marco Quirini and Gian Andrea Doria, whose faces were known even by Turkish pirates sailing the Mediterranean, joined the war councils held on the supreme commander's flagship. With the addition of these two veteran captains, decisions at the war council should have been made in quick succession, but Don Juan's counsel, Lord Requeséns, insisted that they wait for the reconnaissance ship to return. As this was not unreasonable, they waited idly for four days until it arrived.

The Venetian commanders continued to sleep on their ships anchored in the harbor, ready to depart at any moment. They alone refused lodgings in Messina. It was agonizing for them to have the departure date continually postponed with no sense of when the delays would end. Veniero was furious. His deputies may not have been in a position to express it, but they felt the same way.

Famagusta had been able to keep the Turks at bay for over a year, but it was too much to expect the fortress to hold much longer. Venice had committed itself fully to the allied fleet and had no other relief forces or supplies to send to Cyprus. Moreover, as an inevitable result of moving almost its entire navy to Messina, Venice had left the seas near Greece vulnerable to Turkish forces.

The pirate Uluch Ali occupied the vanguard of the Turkish fleet that was heading south from Constantinople. He carried out his duties with enthusiasm, looting the Cretan ports of Canea and Retimo, and even torching a portion of Corfu. He then proceeded north through the Adriatic Sea, attacking one Venetian holding after another along the Dalmatian coast and finally looting the island of Korcula. Korcula was located halfway into the Adriatic, so the Venetian homeland tightened defenses as a precaution. Then came reports that the main Turkish fleet was approaching. These made it impossible to send to Messina the five thousand soldiers that had finally been assembled. Even if such an attempt were made, the soldiers would probably fall victim to the Turkish fleet before they ever made it out of the Adriatic.

All this information was reported in detail to the Venetian commanders in Messina, who could do nothing in response. They couldn't even win any concessions at the war council meetings.

The long-awaited reconnaissance ship returned on September 7th. The Spanish captain and the Venetian first mate reported separately, at the insistence of the Venetians, whose concerns were not unfounded. The two reports were drastically at odds with one another, with one being positive in outlook and the other negative.

The Spanish captain reported that a Turkish fleet consisting of two hundred warships and a hundred transport ships was heading from Corfu towards Lepanto. It was the first time many of those in attendance had even heard the name Lepanto. The Venetians had to describe the sea conditions around Lepanto to those Spaniards and others who were not familiar with the Eastern Mediterranean.

The Venetian first mate reported that the Turkish fleet consisted of a hundred and fifty warships in substantially good condition and approximately a hundred small transport boats. Their weapons appeared to be substandard and considerably inferior to those of the Venetian fleet. Uluch Ali's flotilla, which had apparently been successfully blockaded, was now moving south to rejoin the main fleet. The size of Ali's flotilla and the number of ships currently anchored at Lepanto, however, remained unclear.

The Venetian first mate's report proved to be the more influential of the two among the war council. As a preliminary measure, the council ordered an official pageantry involving all the ships in the allied fleet.

It took place on September 8th. A galley carrying Don Juan and all the ranking officers slowly passed in front of the line of ships that had been deemed fit for battle.

There were 203 galleys, 6 galleasses, 50 small galleys called *fregata*, and 30 large-sail transport ships. A *fregata* was a type of vessel with two masts that flew triangular flags, required thirty rowers, and carried ten soldiers. They were high-speed ships used for reconnaissance and to relay orders. *Fregata*, of course, is the etymological root of the word "frigate." Each convoy typically included two frigates.

It goes without saying that ships participating in the pageantry had all of their sailors and oarsmen aboard, but the full battle contingent of soldiers also had to be present. Various state flags and coats of arms flew on each ship, and all the soldiers, from the Pope's nephew down to common foot soldiers, were lined up on deck, covered in armor and battle gear with their weapons at their sides. Murmurs rose when Don Juan's ship passed. The pageantry that stretched out under the blue Mediterranean sky and across the dark blue sea surely lifted everyone's spirits. The young Don Juan was particularly excited.

Don Juan's sympathies had slowly been shifting, and although that shift became decisive on that day, the two Spaniards ordered by Philip II never to leave the supreme commander's side didn't seem to notice. Lord Requeséns had an inflated view of the authority given to him by the king. Francisco, the priest assigned to be Don Juan's confessor, had an inflated view of the authority given to him by God. Young Don Juan, however, cared more about personal glory than the interests of Spain that had been drilled into him by his half brother in Madrid and by his two advisors during the voyage to Messina.

King Philip II didn't entrust those interests only to Requeséns and Francisco, however. There was also the Genoese Gian Andrea Doria, to whom he had assigned direction of the royal fleet. Doria asked to be the first to speak at the following day's war council.

Doria was still only thirty-two years old. His name, Gian Andrea, may be translated as "Andrea Jr." or "Andrea the Younger." Indeed, he had inherited the mantle from the famous mercenary sea captain Andrea Doria twelve years earlier at the age of twenty. Gian Andrea was a stout young man who, in that respect, bore little resemblance to his uncle, a man who looked like a black falcon even at the age of ninety. Perhaps self-conscious about his prematurely bald head, he never took off his helmet in battle and usually never took off his cap. In the company of Don Juan, however, he did. As a Genoese mercenary commander, he had his own warships, sailors, and soldiers. Spain, which could hardly be called a naval power, had contracted him to provide it with its *de facto* navy.

Warfare for Doria was not just about winning. It was his profession, and it would only come to an end when he died. He, too, had received secret orders from Philip II. His remarks at the war council meeting touched upon two points. First, the Venetian ships were grossly undermanned. They had very little chance of winning a direct engagement with the Turks. Second, it was already mid-September and therefore far too late in the year to pursue the enemy.

The Spaniards also made an issue of the lack of Venetian soldiers. The previous year's epidemic and the five thousand soldiers stuck in Venice meant that Venetian ships only carried eighty soldiers each, whereas Spanish ships carried two hundred each.

The Venetians replied that their oarsmen were free citizens who could substitute as soldiers, but this argument wasn't very convincing when it came to close combat between galleys. The Venetians, eager to set out, didn't want to waste time arguing the point, so when Don Juan made a proposal to rectify the situation they had no choice but to reluctantly accept it.

Don Juan proposed that the Spanish ships lend a portion of their soldiers to the Venetian ships. This would mean adding outsiders to ships otherwise manned only by those loyal to the Venetian Republic: Venetian nobles serving as officers, ordinary Venetians serving as sailors and engineers, and rowers from Dalmatia. Veniero argued that this unity of purpose helped morale and resisted the proposal until the end. But autumn was deepening and even Veniero eventually felt he had no other choice.

Even after this issue was settled, Doria maintained that it was too late to launch that year. Veniero leapt from his seat in a rage. Although the ship they were on was designed for the royal family, the cabin had a low ceiling. Veniero, the tallest man there, looked like he was about to smash through the ceiling.

"Are you suggesting we start over from scratch?" the elderly Venetian officer yelled. He glared one by one at every man in the room, even Don Juan, and added in a low voice that grabbed them all by the collar: "Is there anyone here who wants to drag out this disgraceful farce any longer than it already has?"

No one said a word. Finally, Colonna spoke. "Admiral Veniero, we are allowed to speak freely here, and anyone can speak his mind. But when it comes to making decisions, if two of the three of us have agreed, the remaining one must acquiesce."

"Who gave Doria the right to make any decisions?" Veniero immediately snapped back. He continued by urging them to ship out quickly. Seemingly browbeaten by this forceful declaration, Colonna cautiously announced that he too favored shipping out.

All eyes turned to Don Juan, sitting in the center of the room. If Don Juan voted in opposition, the departure would be decided by a vote of two to one. Given the Spanish side's actions so far, there was every reason to believe he was capable of some perverse display of willfulness. Furthermore, as supreme commander his vote held special weight.

The young man's pale complexion gradually began to redden, and by the time he stood up it was as if his face was on fire.

"We sail," he said.

Everyone in the room stirred at this. The Venetian commanders believed that it had finally been decided.

The twenty-six-year-old prince was not about to forget that he was the one who commanded this alliance of over two hundred ships. His youthful heart burned with the thought that here was a chance to put an end to the Turkish infidels who had carried themselves like the lords of the Mediterranean for nearly the past forty years.

The flames of this ambition had been fanned by the sight of the Venetians' majestic new ship, the galleass. These vessels were altogether like floating fortresses. He found the thought of waiting another year to put this fleet and those ships to use intolerable. Illegitimate prince that he was, there was also no guarantee that he would be put in command next year. He would gamble everything on this one chance.

Requeséns and Francisco stared at him with the glaring eyes of Inquisitors, but this no longer meant anything to the feverish young prince.

The decision having been made, the war council quickly settled on the details. They would set out on September 16th. They chose that date because it was a Sunday, the Christian holy day.

Messina – September 1571

The allied fleet set to depart from Messina Harbor in Sicily was composed of the following: 204 war galleys, 6 galleasses, 50 scout vessels, 30 large transport vessels, 1,815 cannons, 13,000 sailors, 43,500 oarsmen, and 28,000 soldiers.

Most of the large cannons, especially those that fired the largest projectiles, were loaded onto the galleasses. Since the war galleys' effectiveness relied on their mobility, they were not loaded with heavy ordnance. Venice supplied more than half of the war galleys and galleasses, 112 of the 210 total warships.

When it came to the soldiers, however, those serving the King of Spain, though levied from the vassal states of southern Italy and Genoa, numbered three times as many as those from Venice. In other words, the Spanish king paid the salaries of three quarters of the soldiers.

The twenty-eight thousand soldiers were not divided equally among the galleys. In line with Don Juan's proposal, Spanish troops were transferred to the shorthanded Venetian ships, but Malta, Genoa, and Savoy wanted the ships carrying admirals to be boarded by soldiers under their own authority. This resulted in an unavoidable difference in the numbers of soldiers on each galley, ranging from Venetian ships with less than a hundred men, to Spanish ships that averaged a hundred and fifty, to some that exceeded a hundred and eighty.

While many of the Venetian ships were compelled

to take on Spanish soldiers, those vessels that would play a decisive role in the battle fought fiercely to maintain a Venetian-only crew. There wasn't a single foreign soldier on any of the six galleasses. *Capitano Generale de Mare* Veniero's ship and that of Barbarigo, *Provveditore Generale*, along with those of *Provveditore* Quirini and *Provveditore* Canale, also faithfully upheld this policy.

Even after the departure date was set, the war council continued for several days to deliberate. First, they decided to adopt a tripartite battle formation with left and right flanks and a central main fleet. There would also be a reserve flotilla that could rapidly reinforce allied forces in areas where the fighting was particularly fierce.

The first ship position to be decided was that of Supreme Commander Don Juan's flagship, which would serve as the alliance's headquarters. It would assume its place at the very center of the formation, with Venetian admiral Veniero's ship just to its left and Colonna's ship to its immediate right. The Spanish side was adamant at first that Don Juan's vessel had to be flanked by Spanish ships to ensure the royal prince's safety. Lord Requeséns and other ministers of the King of Spain would be aboard those two ships to keep the king's brother in sight at all times during the fighting.

Veniero opposed this. He argued that being flanked by Spanish ships with inexperienced crews would endanger the supreme commander, not make him safer. Colonna suggested that the Spanish ships trail Don Juan's flagship instead, and a compromise was reached. The Spanish escorts would remain within extremely close range of the flagship.

A total of 62 war galleys made up the main force, which included the headquarters. The flagships of the Spanish, Venetian, and papal fleets were concentrated in the center, but the rest of the force became a jostling mass of flagships of every nation competing for a favorable position. The main force also included the flagships of the Maltese Knights of St. John, the Republic of Genoa, and the Duchy of Savoy.

In order to distinguish the three groups, the ships of the main force would fly sky-blue flags, the left flank yellow, and the right flank green. The reserve force would fly white flags.

Agostino Barbarigo had overall command of the 55 war galleys of the left flank flying the yellow ensign. Barbarigo's ship, however, was not positioned in the center, but rather fortified the extreme left edge of the left flank formation. It thus occupied the leftmost position of the entire formation. Admiral Canale's ship came just to the right of Barbarigo's, and Admiral Quirini's ship girded the far right side of the left flank.

Vessels from every country were intermingled in all three of the formation's divisions. As crusaders fighting in the name of Christ, they adopted the name Allied Fleet of the Holy League. The combatants were asked to put aside their allegiances to their countries or knightly orders as proof that they were willing to fight as one. The Venetian Republic, though, had the vast majority of the ships. Though the main force and the right flank were a mix of ships, the left flank was in reality a Venetian fleet. 43 of the 57 ships in this force were Venetian vessels.

Doria commanded the 57 war galleys in the fleet of the right flank. This force also included 25 Venetian ships; once the battle began, these ships, no matter how distasteful they found the proposition, would fight under Doria's command. Doria's ship occupied the position furthest to the right, making the skilled Genoese captain the right flank's first line of defense.

Command of the thirty-galley reserve force in the rear was assigned to the powerful Neapolitan retainer of the Spanish king, the Marquis de Santa Cruz. Spanish vessels outnumbered Venetian sixteen to twelve in this group.

The battle-hardened vessels of Venice and Genoa occupied the most strategic positions. For the same reason, the three veteran ships of the Maltese Knights of St. John were aligned on the extreme right flank of the main force. Supreme Commander Don Juan's ship was surrounded by other flagships, which were large and sturdy. The extreme left and right positions were entrusted to Barbarigo of Venice and Doria of Genoa. This was clearly a formation intended for battle.

Most people, once a decision is made, wish to see it

put into action as quickly as possible. Indeed, everyone except the retainers of the Spanish king eagerly awaited the September 16th departure date.

An eight-ship vanguard, consisting of six war galleys accompanied by two light scout ships, was first to leave the harbor. The air rang with repeated cannon salutes fired from the fortress at the mouth of the harbor.

During the day, these eight ships would be responsible for reconnaissance over an area of thirty square nautical miles, and by night they would sail ten nautical miles behind the main fleet. When the battle began, all but the light scout vessels were to move into their set positions within the main force.

The six galleasses followed the vanguard out of the harbor. There was no wind early that morning, so they were towed out by scout ships. These six "floating batteries" were to move to the frontmost line as soon as they encountered the enemy. By wreaking havoc on the enemy with their cannon fire, they would create the perfect opening for the war galleys, which were in fact the backbone of the force.

With Doria's flagship in the lead, the fleet of the right flank departed the harbor six nautical miles behind the galleasses. The 57 ships of this formation, green flags flying from their prows, left the harbor in columns of three.

Then came the main force, which consisted of the 56 warships that remained after six had departed in the vanguard. This group was particularly ostentatious because of the concentration of flagships. Veniero and Colonna's ships flanked Don Juan's with their prows in perfect alignment. The oars of Don Juan's ship were gleaming white, while those of Veniero's were completely crimson. The ships cut through the waves, sky-blue flags flying.

The 55 ships comprising the left flank followed behind. The crimson-colored Venetian flagship bearing Agostino Barbarigo, commanding admiral of the left flank, led the way. The last of the 55 ships to leave the harbor was the ship of Admiral Quirini. Upon meeting the enemy at sea, Barbarigo's ship would stop and wait for Quirini's ship to close in on the right, completing the battle formation of the left flank by anchoring both ends. Yellow flags flew from the prows of each of these ships.

It was already close to midday when the Marquis de Santa Cruz led the rear guard out of the harbor. Since the winds had risen by this time, the thirty ships flying white flags pursued the rest of the fleet at full speed. Thirty sailing ships led by Marquis Davalos also left the harbor using the favorable winds to their advantage. Even though they weren't being pulled by galleys, they quickly disappeared into the distance like a flock of white water-fowl.

Philip II, angered by the unexpected developments, dispatched a letter to Don Juan ordering him to return home. It arrived in Messina three days after the fleet left port.

Ionian Sea – September 1571

While the allied fleet may have left Messina in an orderly fashion, it fell into disarray upon arriving at the southern tip of the Italian peninsula, where it attempted to pass through the fast-flowing tides of the straits. The handling of the ships depended of course on each crew's competence, but problems arose because each country's flagship wanted the honor of passing first. One such dispute arose between the flagship of Savoy and that of the Maltese Knights of St. John.

According to the rules of passage the Knights' ship, stationed on the right edge of the main force, was entitled to go first. The crew of the ship from Savoy, however, didn't recognize that privilege, forcing Supreme Commander Don Juan to hand down a judgment on what was, after all, a very trivial matter. He ordered the flagship of Savoy to go first. Savoy had only provided three ships, but Duke Urbino and his military attachés were aboard their flagship. To show respect for Savoy and Duke Urbino, Don Juan directed their ship just to the right of Colonna, in other words, right alongside the flagships of the commanding admirals.

The fleet fell out of order not only because of incidents such as this, but also because of differences in speed arising from the differing abilities of Italian sailors, products of a long maritime tradition, and Spanish sailors, who were less skilled. At the very least, however, the tripartite division of right flank, main force, and left flank was maintained.

The weather was still favorable on September 18th, the third day after departing from Messina, when the fleet rounded the southern tip of the Italian peninsula—the toe of the Italian boot—and entered the Ionian Sea. The fleet of over two hundred ships made a spectacular sight, yet there wasn't a soul along the shoreline to appreciate it. Most people had long since fled to the mountains to escape years of victimization by Muslim pirates. Uluch Ali, who was enjoying great military success in the Turkish navy, had been born in this region in the fishing village of Castella. He had been carried off and sold into slavery by Turkish pirates when he was sixteen. It was said that not a single town along the southern Italian coast had escaped the Islamic pirates' depredations.

The allied fleet then proceeded northeast from the boot's tip towards its arch. They arrived at a place the sailors call *Capo della Colonna* (Cape of the Columns) on the morning of September 20th. It was the fifth day of their voyage, which had thus far gone smoothly.

Don Juan felt the smooth passage had given them some leeway in terms of time. He ordered all the ships to rest there, although people more familiar with the sea were opposed. They said the skies looked ominous, but Don Juan wouldn't listen. In the end, the entire fleet dropped anchor to rest in the shade of the mountains. Don Juan dispatched a relay vessel to Veniero's ship to ask him about reinforcing the soldiers on the Venetian ships with six hundred troops who had been stationed at the nearby city of Crotone.

Veniero feared that this would be a waste of precious time, so he immediately refused without consulting his second-in-command, Barbarigo. Veniero wanted to rush to Cyprus's aid as soon as possible. He sent back a proposal to Don Juan that they set out again at full speed across the Ionian Sea towards the island of Zante. Before Don Juan could reply, the weather took a sudden turn for the worse.

That night, a fierce rainstorm assailed the allied fleet. Strong winds from the north swelled the sea, sending massive waves that completely engulfed the ships and flooded the hulls. For the first time, fear of the sea broke the spirits of the nobles and knights whose proud bearing on land was unshakable. On the 20th and the 21st, the sea showed no signs of settling down. The fleet had completely fallen out of any kind of formation, and the sailors fought the chaos by chaining their ships together in a desperate struggle to avoid drifting apart.

Calm finally returned to the seas halfway through the night of the 21st. Veniero's proposal, however, of racing east across the Ionian Sea—in other words, going directly into the open sea with no possibility of stopping at port—had been roundly rejected. With the prospect of several days of rough seas ahead, the nobles and knights appealed to the supreme commander to follow a course along the coastline. Nonetheless, even they didn't object to making a line directly for the "heel" of the peninsula at San Maria di Leuca instead of proceeding via Taranto, deep in the "arch." The seas had calmed enough that the sailing ships could unfurl their sails.

On the morning of September 23rd, the fleet could see the promontory of San Maria di Leuca in the distance. From this point onward, even those most afraid of the sea had to resign themselves to the impossibility of remaining within sight of land: doing so would have meant circumnavigating the entire Adriatic Sea. Their only choice was to head east through the open sea until they reached Corfu. Blessed with smooth sailing, the outline of the island of Corfu became visible above the horizon on the morning of September 24th. They were now on the Greek side of the Ionian Sea.

A number of small islands were scattered in the seas around Corfu. The fleet waited off the island of Samothrace for the trailing ships, while Veniero's vessel alone pressed on to Corfu, an important base for the Venetian Republic; it was essential that the Venetians there greet Supreme Commander Don Juan with an appropriate show of gratitude. Veniero went ahead in order to make the necessary preparations.

The seas once again grew rough and the fleet off Samothrace had difficulty staying in formation. The ocean here was relatively shallow, so chilly winds from the northwest easily blew up waves. The fleet couldn't enter Corfu's harbor until September 26th.

The fortress at the entrance to the harbor greeted them with cannon salutes. The docks had been cleared of the usual trading vessels to make room for the vast armada now arriving.

Corfu was responsible for defending the access route to the Adriatic Sea, also known as the "Gulf of Venice." The towering fortress the Corfiots had built on the harbor cape was so impressive that it took the breath away of those unfamiliar with the finer points of maritime defense. The mainland facing Corfu appeared dimly purple in the distance, with the closest points seemingly right before one's eyes. That was Turkish territory.

Traces of Uluch Ali's attacks were evident in Corfu, but the harbor, guarded by the great fortress, was safe. Turkish troops had landed on weakly defended parts of the island but had only been able to torch those areas before being forced to withdraw.

In Corfu, the leaders of the alliance were able to gather the most recent and accurate information concerning the Turkish fleet. They learned that the large fleet led by Ali Pasha had not yet departed Greek waters. Including the smaller boats, this fleet numbered close to three hundred ships. Uluch Ali's flotilla had apparently already merged with it. The main force was said to be anchored at Lepanto, separated from Corfu by a voyage of only a few days. Suddenly, the enemy felt very close indeed.

At Corfu, Barbarigo picked up a number of letters

from Flora that had been collecting there for some time since they could not be forwarded to Messina. He read them again and again during whatever spare time he could find. For a man away at war, the peace and tranquility conveyed by the prosaic chronicles of the daily lives of mother and son created a real sense of nostalgia.

He wrote back to her. His letters this time, however, were not the detailed recountings that they had been. Ever since joining Don Juan in Messina he hadn't had the time or the energy to write to her, and after a month of not writing, it was difficult to resume the habit. Especially now, knowing that the enemy was in Lepanto and that battle was in the offing, he couldn't just list his quotidian doings as if the routine would continue forever.

That said, he wasn't really sure what he should write instead. He ended up rambling on endlessly about the many things on his mind. He could only smile bitterly as he reread the resulting letter, which had an extremely warm tone by his standards, but was also extremely trite.

After telling them to stay warm, he ran out of things to say. Indeed, the entire letter was packed with such commonplaces. It occurred to him that he might be unable to write until he returned once again to Corfu, so he added, "Don't worry if a letter doesn't come for a while." He closed with, "Be sure to take care of yourselves," but then noticed that he had written that same sentence at least three times. He laughed out loud, causing his servant to open his door to see what was going on.

His letter would probably be sent to Venice on the same fast boat that had delivered a statement from the Venetian senate to the fleet in Corfu; it would take about ten days to reach Venice. The letter from the senate had read: "The people of the Republic of Venice stand united behind you. Fight the enemy with all of your strength."

Grecian Waters – October 1571

The Spaniards proposed a new plan at the war council in Corfu. In their minds, the great size of the Turkish fleet made victory in a sea battle rather unlikely. They therefore suggested occupying Negroponte in Greece for the time being.

Veniero, once again, was loudly opposed. The enemy was right next door; what was the point of bypassing them to reach Negroponte? Tensions between the Spaniards and the Venetians were running high.

Despite this, they were able to agree to leave Corfu and go to Igoumenitsa, a harbor on the coast directly opposite Corfu. That was at the beginning of October. They were leaving Igoumenitsa and heading south past Paxos toward San Maura Island when more trouble arose.

Animosity among the leadership invariably filters down to the rank and file. These feelings compound the soldiers' usual level of discontent, and what admirals express with words the common soldiers wind up expressing with their fists. The Venetians and the Spanish troops hadn't gotten along very well since the fleet had assembled in Messina. The tension began to boil especially after Don Juan proposed that Spanish troops be stationed on the undermanned Venetian ships.

Spain was a great power in the Mediterranean, and was still on its way up. Venice, on the other hand, had already seen its best days. The fact that Venice was putting all its resources into this allied fleet clearly showed that it felt its survival was riding on the outcome. This was not the case with Spain.

The people of a rising power tend to look down on those whose glories are in the past. Particularly in a case like this, when they know how badly they are needed, the upstarts' behavior is often intolerable. An incident on one of the Venetian ships is a case in point.

The most important people aboard a ship at sea are the men navigating and sailing it. The war galleys had triangular sails, and every time the direction of the wind changed the sailors had to lower the yardarms and either change their direction to correspond to the wind or change to a different type of sail. Then they had to raise those long, heavy yardarms up along the masts. On those occasions, the passageway between the oarsmen, who were lined up along the gunwales, became a battleground dedicated to accomplishing those operations skillfully and efficiently.

The sailors were, of course, accustomed to this, and the skills of those assigned to warships were particularly well honed. The width of the central aisle measured no more than a meter, so people loitering there with nothing to do just got in the way. Even if they were royalty, they could expect a shower of angry obscenities from sailors trying to do their jobs.

The Spanish commanders, unfamiliar with life at sea, didn't know that this was how things worked. Besides, there was no one with less to do than a soldier on a sailing warship; his job only began when the ship engaged the enemy. Although the ranking officers might spend their free time refining their battle strategy, the junior officers and enlisted men had trouble figuring out how to pass the time. They were lucky if they could complete a voyage without getting into any trouble.

Venetians knew how to deal with this. Even if a man was on board in the role of soldier, he would spend his time assisting the sailors at their work. A few of these soldiers were so proficient they could easily have switched jobs.

Spain and France, however, were not naval powers, and knights from those countries were exceptionally proud of belonging to a class that bore arms; it would never have occurred to them to assist the sailors. Even if they had tried, the help of an amateur was more hindrance than help. The Spanish troops, thoughtlessly going back and forth between the prow and the bridge on the Venetian ships, crowding the center aisle, eventually became a source of trouble.

The crowding alone was enough to anger the Venetians, who had been tolerating it ever since they had set sail from Messina. The Spanish troops' arrogance only made matters worse. One day a Spanish army captain strolled aimlessly down the center aisle without any regard for bustling activity around him and was promptly told off by a Venetian sailor.

The captain wouldn't let the offense go unanswered. He and three of his comrades ganged up on the sailor, who lay dead on the deck by the time they walked away.

This caused an uproar among the other sailors and oarsmen. The Venetian soldiers also rushed over, and a melee erupted. When he got the news, Veniero had himself rowed over to the ship in question.

After being briefed by the ship's captain, Veniero had the four suspects brought forth and immediately sentenced them to death in an act of summary justice. His reasoning was that anyone on a Venetian ship, even a foreigner, was under the jurisdiction of the commander in chief of the Venetian navy. As a punishment for causing a breakdown in discipline in a time of war, the death penalty was both reasonable and legal. The oarsmen, who had been waiting eagerly, carried out the sentence. The four Spanish soldiers were hung side by side from a yardarm.

When Don Juan found out about this, he flew into a rage.

His consciousness of his position as supreme commander of the allied fleet had only grown stronger with time. That was precisely why he had gone against his own advisors' objections, even against the wishes of his half brother the king, in favor of seeking out the enemy. Veniero had executed Spaniards without so much as a word of consultation with him. Don Juan took this as an act of rank insubordination and a challenge to his authority as supreme commander.

Don Juan didn't summon Veniero, but rather Barbarigo. Pale with rage, he told Barbarigo, "Veniero will meet with the same punishment as those Spanish soldiers hanging from the yardarm."

In his usual unflappable tone, Barbarigo crisply replied, "Your Highness, should anything of that nature occur, the entire fleet of Venice would have no choice but to withdraw from the alliance."

This was enough to stop Don Juan from uttering another word. Colonna, who was in attendance, once again stepped in as mediator and proposed that Veniero be excluded from the war council. After some considera-tion, Don Juan assented. Barbarigo also found this acceptable. From then on, Barbarigo would function as Venice's principal representative at the council.

The allied fleet continued southward. Information arrived two days later that helped unite the nearly frac-tured spirit of the allied fleet, returning it to what it had been the day the fleet departed Messina.

A small galley on its way home to Venice from Cyprus brought news of the fall of Famagusta. The entire fleet was filled with anger and astonishment. The fall was said to have occurred on August 24th, one day after Don Juan arrived in Messina. The reason the news had arrived so late was because the defenders of the fortress had all been killed. There had been literally no one to deliver it.

The fighting in the waters off Famagusta had been increasing in intensity since May. A tight blockade by the

Turkish navy was preventing all ships, even those from Crete, from getting close. Venetians living in Crete, though, had at least been able to get information by secretly entering via the southern coast of Cyprus away from Famagusta. The news that Famagusta had been defeated after a year of fierce fighting came from those Venetians, some of whom had posed as Greeks to enter the area just after its fall.

The defending army had run out of rations, weapons, and gunpowder, and there had been no hope of reinforcements. The yearlong siege ended when Mustafa Pasha of the Turkish army offered the defenders safe passage off the island as a condition of their surrender. Bragadino, the leader of the besieged army, was told that the safety of the lives of his Venetian troops and other residents would be absolutely guaranteed, so he finally accepted the terms.

The Turkish general, however, did not keep his promise. Once the fort was opened, every Venetian, from noblemen down to shopkeepers, was first tortured and then killed. As for the Greeks who had joined the defenders, the very old and the very young were killed while the rest were sold into slavery. For Bragadino, who was forced to witness all of this, a very special death was prepared as punishment for having resisted the Turks for an entire year.

While the Venetian commander was still alive, the Turks first flayed the skin from his entire body. They then repeatedly dunked him into the sea. Even so, Bragadino didn't stop breathing. It wasn't until they cut off his head that he blessedly breathed his last. The Turks stitched together his flayed skin, stuffed it with straw, and sewed on his severed head. This mannequin made from human skin was sent to the Turkish capital of Constantinople and pilloried in the public square, after which it was sent to be publicly exhibited in every province of the vast Ottoman Empire.

The members of the allied fleet no longer thought of themselves as Spaniards and Venetians. Faces contorted with fury and grief, they swore to exact revenge on the barbaric Turkish infidels. Not surprisingly, emotions ran particularly high on the Venetian ships. Even oarsmen who were convicted criminals serving aboard to earn reduced sentences burned with rage, beating their chests and grunting through clenched teeth. Now there was nobody left who suggested turning back.

The members of the fleet quickly and skillfully completed inspections of their ships. They finalized gunner and crossbow archer positions as well as the formation of the fleet itself. They continued southward, ready to battle the enemy wherever they might find him.

Lepanto – October 1571

The wind was weak, so most of the ships relied on their oarsmen. Even at night, no order came to stop. Stillness ruled so perfectly that the beautiful twinkling stars could be appreciated, yet the point of running at night was not to enjoy the celestial lights; the sailors looked intently up at them to determine their bearings, and gauged the distance between each ship by looking at the large lanterns hoisted on the prow and stern of every vessel. They headed south past the opening to the bay of Preveza and along the west coast of San Maura Island. The ancient hero Odysseus's island of Ithaca, and then Kefalonia, would soon appear in the south.

The chain of islands in that area belonged to the Venetian Republic. The islands starting from Corfu and extending to Kefalonia, moreover, were so close to the Greek mainland, which was Turkish territory, that they were in fact Venice's frontline defensive posts. They had to be wary. The eyes of Turkish reconnaissance ships were hidden away somewhere among the silhouettes of the islands.

Silence was ordered on all ships. Only the creaking of the oars and the sound of the prow cutting through the waves disturbed the quiet of the sea. The sailors even extinguished the torches on the ship's bridges that were not necessary for gauging the distances. Nonetheless, the armada of over two hundred ships, each with a blazing lantern rising up over its prow and stern, illuminated the entire surrounding sea. The Turkish reconnaissance ships following this silent fleet thought they were facing an enemy greater in numbers than they actually were.

The Greek name for Lepanto is Nafpaktos. Venetians had controlled the area for many years and had used the port as a refuge for ships in trouble. Now, as in the past, it is little more than a small village. The walls that still encircle the hillsides were built by the Venetians. The harbor is deep within the Gulf of Patras, which divides the Greek mainland from the Peloponnesian peninsula; Corinth is due east. The Venetians had used it as a safe harbor for good reason, as any fleet was completely protected in there and had no chance of being lured out westward into the Gulf of Patras.

It was October and thus already time, especially with war looming, for ordinary sea vessels to start heading to their winter ports. Lepanto could accommodate roughly three hundred ships, which, to the Venetian sea captains who knew these waters as well as any Muslim pirate, meant that the Turkish fleet could conceivably be that size. This was their one worry.

The Turkish commanders in the harbor at Lepanto were themselves divided about how to deal with the alliance.

They had been told that the allied fleet was at least the same size, if not larger, than theirs. More than a few of them insisted it was prudent to stay where they were and avoid fighting that fall. Many of the pirates also advocated waiting. They may not have contributed that many ships to the fleet, but in terms of seamanship and prowess in combat they were the backbone of the Turkish navy. Both Uluch Ali and Suluk, better known by his nickname "Scirocco," strongly advocated waiting.

The Turks knew that Western Europe was not unified—the events of the previous year had proved that. Although the Europeans appeared to have ironed out their differences for the time being, next year could be a different story. Those opposed to fighting believed that they should not engage the allied fleet in even a single battle as autumn deepened. It was not only the pirate leaders, however, who felt this way; ministers of the Turkish court accompanying Grand Admiral Ali Pasha held the same opinion. Many of them were court ministers who had served the empire under the previous sultan, Suleiman, and belonged to the moderate faction represented by Grand Vizier Sokullu in Constantinople. These seasoned ministers believed that since Cyprus had been taken and the object of the war accomplished, there was no point in brashly challenging the Christians. Ali Pasha, however, was of a younger generation and eager to engage in battle.

This was the first time that Ali Pasha had been entrusted with such a great fleet. He wasn't a politician entangled in the divide in the Turkish court between the faction that wanted to continue Suleiman's policies and the much more aggressive faction that followed the new sultan. He was a pureblooded Turk highly conscious of his role as a member of the grand Ottoman Empire. The battle flag, embroidered in gold with a passage from the Koran and personally presented to him by Sultan Selim, was never far from his thoughts. This sacred flag had never flown anywhere except atop the mast of the flagship from which he commanded his vast fleet. He couldn't bear to think how shameful it would be for him, as a full-blooded Turkish admiral, to return home without ever having flown that flag in battle.

The court ministers opposed to engaging the enemy were Christians who had converted to Islam as children. Even though they were the appointed governors of Alexandria and Algiers as well as pirate leaders, Scirocco and Uluch Ali were converts to Islam. Ali Pasha felt that the blood running through the veins of such people was different from his own. He was willing to stake everything on this one battle—even the lives of his two young sons, whom he had brought along. The converts didn't possess that kind of resolve.

Ali Pasha had another reason for insisting on battle despite the opposition of all the other court ministers and commanders. When he sailed out of Constantinople, he had been given a letter from the sultan that directed him to crush the Christian fleet at any cost. Because so many of his advisors disagreed with him, Ali Pasha dispatched a messenger to relay the opinions of the dissenters, asking his lord for reconfirmation. Sultan Selim's position was the same as before.

Ali Pasha addressed the ministers and pirate leaders. He told them that their Greek informants had numbered the enemy fleet, including transport vessels, at no more that two hundred and fifty. "Our side is superior!" he said.

Uluch Ali, the governor of Algiers, formally rebutted that assertion. "Superiority is not determined by the number of ships. This is a matter of armaments. Our ships are generally smaller than theirs and we are clearly inferior to the enemy in terms of firepower— especially when up against those six monster ships. Counting those as if they were normal galleys would be a fatal mistake. Furthermore, Sebastiano Veniero is leading the Venetian navy. Have no doubt that the Venetian fleet under him will hit us with all their might as soon as they see us."

Ali Pasha looked at the Italian-born pirate, a man nearly the same age as himself, with an expression of the utmost scorn. In a harsh tone he replied, "It is said that Barbarosa, a pirate of a generation ago, was extended a bribe by Charles, the Spanish king at the time. I have heard that the present king, Philip II, is also inviting some formerly Christian pirates to reconvert to Christianity. I do pray your reservations are not proof that you have accepted such an invitation."

Uluch Ali said nothing. Actually, this rumor had also been circulating within the Christian fleet. Emboldened by Uluch Ali's silence, the Turkish grand admiral concluded with what felt like the final stroke of the sword: "They say the leader of the Christian coalition is the younger brother of the king of Spain. Since the brother of the king has taken the trouble to sail out for battle, we cannot simply lower and furl our banners. Boldly confronting the enemy is the only action appropriate to the Ottoman Empire."

No one presented opposition any longer. They decided that the Turkish fleet would leave the harbor of Lepanto in hopes of a sea battle with the approaching Christian fleet.

The Turks now had to decide on an appropriate formation for a sea battle.

The main force of the Turkish fleet commanded by Ali Pasha himself would engage the opposing main force, which was undoubtedly led by the brother of the Spanish king. Ali Pasha's fleet was composed of 96 war galleys, and his flagship was specially outfitted with an attack force of 400 elite Janissaries. The flanks of the flagship would be guarded by the ships carrying his ministers. The right flank would consist of 55 war galleys and take on the Christian fleet's left flank. It was placed under the command of the governor of Alexandria, the pirate leader Scirocco. The 94 war galleys assigned to the left flank would come up against the enemy's right flank. Command was entrusted to Uluch Ali, the governor of Algiers.

Scirocco and Uluch Ali's ships were given the positions at the far right and the far left of the entire battle formation. The Turkish fleet was spreading out its naval veterans in order to brace the entire force. Thirty ships were held back as a reserve, led by another pirate captain, Dragut. The reserve, however, mostly consisted of small galleys.

The Grand Admiral Ali Pasha gave the order to wait for the early morning of October 7th, when the entire fleet would leave Lepanto, enter the Gulf of Patras, and engage the enemy. That was two days away.

The islands of Ithaca and Kefalonia had probably been one island in the distant past. The two appear as if they could fit snugly into each other and are separated by a narrow strait of only about three hundred meters. Towering cliffs loom over the water at Ithaca, bringing to mind the epithet "rocky Ithaca" from Homer's *Odyssey*. The strong and capricious gusts that buffet the island bring to mind another of Homer's recurring terms for Ithaca: "windy."

For some reason, the Venetian sailors called this strait the "Valley of Alexandria." The allied fleet was waiting impatiently in the waters leading to this strait for the return of the last reconnaissance ship they had sent off. The ship returned with the news that the enemy fleet nestled in the waters off Lepanto's harbor was showing signs of preparation for battle.

"The enemy is leaving his lair!"

The members of the war council felt as if their last

remaining worry had been removed. All that was left was to head into battle.

Wind blew in the "Valley of Alexandria" even when everywhere else it was still. A slight breeze elsewhere became a gale in the narrow strait. Passing through the strait, however, did have an advantage. Ithaca and Kefalonia were both Venetian territory, and Kefalonia possessed a safe harbor. Furthermore, there was only a slight breeze blowing near the strait on October 6th that year.

The galleys and the galleasses furled all their sails and started to head south using their oars. The sailing ships were towed by the galleys. In fact, all the ships made the passage through the strait during that one day. When they emerged from the "Valley of Alexandria," a strong wind was blowing from the east.

As if blown away by that wind, the black of night faded and the sun gradually rose in the east. October 7, 1571 had arrived. Those who had stolen a brief snatch of sleep cast their sleepy eyes eastward—then, after a slight shiver from the cold air, rose to their feet.

Lepanto – October 7, 1571 – Morning

The plan called for them to wait at the mouth of the Gulf of Patras in a bow-shaped formation. They were certain that the dark line growing on the eastern horizon was the Turkish fleet. The cargo transports headed off to the west to wait in the harbor of Kefalonia. The rest of the ships lined up from south to north in the tripartite formation they had used when passing through the "Valley of Alexandria." The strong headwinds, however, made their passage more difficult than they had hoped and resulted in some delays.

The Turkish fleet was also slow in passing through the narrow strait connecting the respective bays of Lepanto and Patras. While they did have a favorable wind behind them and were running with full sails, they were still a large armada of three hundred ships. Since the allied fleet lay directly to the west and the eastern sky was still so dimly lit, it was impossible for them to make out the enemy fleet. In this case, the Turks' numerical superiority also made it easier for things to fall into confusion, though in the end the fleet did finally complete passage into the Gulf of Patras.

The Christian fleet spotted the enemy immediately. Against the background of the brightening eastern sky, the approaching ships with raised sails looked exactly like a silhouette drawing. At first only one ship could be made out, but that soon multiplied into two, and then four, until finally they filled the entire field of vision.

In the history of naval warfare, the largest and indeed the final battle between galleys was the Battle of Lepanto. As in most great battles, whether on land or sea, winning was not simply a matter of spotting the enemy and immediately engaging in battle. There were some differences between them, but both naval fleets had at least 200 ships, over 13,000 sailors, more than 40,000 oarsmen and as many as 30,000 soldiers. The only major difference was the number of cannons, with the Muslim side possessing 750 to the Christians' 1,800.

This was a face-to-face confrontation involving over 500 ships and 170,000 men. Getting into formation was itself a challenge.

The sun had risen and there wasn't a cloud in the sky. The eastern wind called the Levante continued to gust as the Turkish fleet sailed into the Gulf of Patras.

The waters where the allied fleet lay in wait were bounded to the north by shoals, but to the south it opened out to the western tip of the Peloponnesian peninsula. The mercenary captain Doria, commanding the right flank of the allied fleet, was responsible for that sector.

Leading the left flank of the Turkish fleet—which was slowly growing larger before Doria's eyes—came a ship flying a flag he had seen many times in the past. All the Christians living on the Mediterranean knew the pirate Uluch Ali by name, even without reference to his official title, Governor of Algiers. Doria realized now whom he would be facing, and the pirate, no doubt, had a similar realization.

Doria veered right. This was open sea and his enemy was Uluch Ali. Doria was trying to circle around and pin Uluch Ali from the right.

When Doria's ship moved, all the other ships in the right flank followed suit. As a result, an alarming gap opened in the Christian fleet between the right flank and the main force. Six galleasses had been stationed in pairs on the front line directly ahead of the left flank, main force, and right flank. The two that had been in front of the right flank were no longer in proper position. Galleasses couldn't maneuver as well as the galleys, so these two were now positioned in the gap between the right flank and the main force.

To occupy the middle part of a bow formation, the main force of sixty-two ships assumed positions recessed behind the left flank and right flanks.

Don Juan's flagship was in the center, with Veniero and his Venetian flagship on his left, and Colonna and his papal flagship on his right. The flagships of Savoy, Florence, and various other contingents filled out the core of flagships that secured Don Juan's flanks. The leader of the Maltese Knights of the Order of St. John commanded the flagship on the far right of the main force and the far left was held by the flagship of the Republic of Genoa.

Like the Muslim fleet, the Christian fleet had braced the extreme left and right positions with experienced sea captains, but they were not able to place similarly experienced naval officers everywhere along the tripartite battle formation.

The two ships containing the palace guard of the Spanish king had their prows virtually attached to the stern of Don Juan's ship. Additionally, the reserve flotilla led by the Marquis de Santa Cruz held its position directly behind the main force, the reinforcement of which was its main priority. In truth, as retainer of the King of Spain, the Marquis de Santa Cruz had no concern other than protecting Don Juan's ship.

Two galleasses had positioned themselves in front of the main force. Francesco Duodo, the overall commander of the six galleasses, was in one of them. The remaining galleass captains were from the Venetian aristocracy, but in actuality the power displayed by the galleasses owed to the Venetian middle class, its engineers and master shipbuilders.

Barbarigo's crimson ship was at the far end of the left flank. River-fed shoals and small islands could be seen to the left of their formation. To Barbarigo's immediate right was the ship of veteran sea captain da Canale. Securing the far right of the left flank was the ship of Marco Quirini, who was no stranger to fighting the Turks.

The captains of the primarily Venetian left flank

knew from the approaching battle flag that their opponent would be the pirate Scirocco. Barbarigo had faced
off with Scirocco several times while stationed in
Cyprus. Canale and Quirini, who had both spent a long
tour in Crete, had often been tormented by this particular foe. From the deck of his craft, Marco Quirini
shouted toward Barbarigo in their shared Venetian
dialect, "We've got the enemy!" Barbarigo waved back to
him in acknowledgement.

Assuming the battle formation required a great deal
of time and effort, but it came as no surprise.

The sun was rising in the east, which meant the
allied fleet would be fighting with the sun in their eyes.
They had to contend with the additional disadvantage of
having the wind to their faces. The fact that the Turkish
fleet took so long getting into formation despite their
favorable winds helped compensate for these
disadvantages. An even greater stroke of good fortune
would arrive around noon.

When the sun was at its highest point in the sky, the
wind suddenly stopped. All the tightly stretched sails
high on the masts of the Turkish ships went completely
limp. Nearly all the men of the allied fleet sensed at that
moment that they had gained the upper hand. Supreme
Commander Don Juan boarded a skiff and passed in
front of the prows of the entire fleet. He wasn't conduct-
ing a final inspection. With the enthusiasm one would
expect from a twenty-six-year-old, he intended to rouse

the troops.

The tall figure of the young supreme commander was encased in shining steel armor. He exhorted the men at the top of his voice, holding aloft a silver cross in his right hand where there normally would have been a sword. A loud roar rose from the ranks of the nobles, knights, and soldiers lining the decks, and even from the oarsmen. Waves of cheers swept from the left flank to the right.

When Don Juan arrived in front of Veniero's ship, he recognized the old admiral standing amidst the shower of frenzied screams and shouted to him in Italian, "For what cause do we fight?"

Veniero was wearing his armor but no helmet; his white hair streamed in the sea breeze. He held a crossbow in his right hand and answered in a loud voice, "Because we must, Your Highness, that is all!"

Don Juan completed a full pass in front of the entire fleet and then had all of the ships lower their state flags and assorted coats of arms. Then, high on the mast of Don Juan's flagship, he raised the consecrated flag of the alliance. It had a pattern embroidered in silver thread on a field of sky blue damask. In the center was the image of the crucified Christ, at whose feet were embroidered the insignias of the central participants of the Holy League: Spain, the Papal States, and the Republic of Venice. This grand battle flag could be seen from everywhere along the battle line.

Everyone on deck—the eminent nobles and knights in resplendent armor, the soldiers carrying crossbows or guns, the sailors manning the helm, the oarsmen at their rowing platforms, even the untrustworthy prisoners who had been promised freedom after the battle had been fought—all dropped to their knees and offered up a prayer to God. This was a crusade. They were fighting for the glory of Christ the Lord. In that moment, perhaps the purest element of the Counter-Reformation crystallized into a single sentiment. All other thoughts and concerns dropped away; all that remained was a single-minded desire to face the enemy.

All hands returned to their stations. The oarsmen picked up their oars and the sailors took their positions under the furled sails or by the helm in the stern. The artillerymen tended their cannons, while the gunners and the crossbowmen lined up along the left and right gunwales. The knights also took up formation, swords and spears in hand, in the center aisles.

The captains on the Venetian ships also served as their infantry commanders; they led the attacks from the prows of their ships. It was standard on the ships of other countries for the captain to stand at the head of the stern bridge, in order to be near the helmsman. The Venetian captains, however, sent orders to their helmsman by relaying dispatches down the center aisle.

After the prayer, the ships were once again allowed to raise their state flags and coats of arms from their bridges. But the silver cross of the alliance was the only flag to be flown high atop the mast, while the yellow, blue, and green pennants waved from the prows to identify the battle groupings. The point of giving prominence to the alliance flag was for the men to set aside their parochial differences and stand united in their Christianity.

The preparations were now complete on the Christian side, where ninety thousand men awaited the signal to begin battle.

The Muslim fleet had also finished its own preparations.

It, too, took up a bow-shaped formation reminiscent of the crescent moon, symbol of Islam. The men making up the fleet hailed from Greece, Syria, Egypt, and North Africa, but since all were subjects of the Ottoman Empire, there were no national flags. There were only flags with various combinations of red, white, and green backgrounds with white, red, or yellow crescent moons. There were also a number of distinctive pirate flags.

The grand battle flag with a Koranic verse stitched in gold flew high atop the mast of Grand Admiral Ali Pasha's flagship. This sacred flag had been specially brought from Mecca just for this occasion. The verse on the flag read: *Allah rewards believers who perform good works for Him and His prophet Mohammed.*

This was a holy war for the Muslims as well, a clash between the cross and the crescent.

Lepanto – October 7, 1571 – Afternoon

It was a little past noon when the cannon sounded from Ali Pasha's flagship. Don Juan's ship immediately answered with its own cannon.

The cannons of the six galleasses on the front line belched fire almost simultaneously in a thunderous signal for battle. They made several direct hits on the Turkish warships, which were advancing with their oars. After this initial round, the "floating batteries" of the Christian forces continued the bombardment. They made direct hits again and again on a number of ships, some of which caught fire and listed in the water. The Turks' crescent-shaped battle formation was broken in several places as they attempted to advance. Seeing the Turkish formation break up like this greatly lifted the spirits of the alliance fighters waiting behind the galleasses.

The Turkish ships seemed to be trying to get past the galleasses as quickly as possible. Christian slaves were chained to the decks, and the slave drivers whipped them like madmen to make the ships move at top speed. The Turkish ships started to surge past the galleasses. The gun ports on both the left and right gunwales of the "floating batteries," however, were open, and they certainly weren't silent.

The battle formation of the Turkish fleet was in complete disarray, but the relatively small size of their ships saved them from falling prey to the large cannons. The ships that did make it through the galleasses plunged ahead toward the allied fleet, which was also advancing.

It would take time for the galleasses that had been bypassed to change position. Now the galleys were the main players.

The close fighting that began was much like a land battle.

Along the alliance's middle and left lines, oars of the opposed navies locked together. On ships that managed to get close to the enemy, men vied for the chance to be the first to make the assault, ready to leap over the oarsmen's heads if necessary.

Janissaries were poised on the prow of Ali Pasha's ship, which was making a dash for Don Juan's craft. These Janissaries made up the sultan's palace guard and were reputed to be the fiercest and bravest fighters in the Ottoman army. They were fully prepared to board the enemy's ship at any moment.

A dull thud filled the air when the bows of the two ships smashed together. Neither of the two sea marshal's ships had made any attempt to soften the impact, crushed bows be damned.

Veniero used this opportunity to move his ship into position and lock oars with a Turkish ship that had approached alongside Ali Pasha's vessel. The momentum from this collision pushed the Turkish ship right into Ali Pasha's, forcing the two to lock oars. Now both Turkish ships were immobilized. The Janissaries, however, were not in the least fazed. Prohibited from having wives or families, they were warriors to the core—having their backs to the wall just made them fight that much harder.

Similar skirmishes were breaking out all throughout the main force. Veniero's ship alone was taking on three enemy vessels, and the Roman aristocracy aboard Colonna's ship displayed similar valiance. The battle line had fallen into complete disarray with whirlwinds of fierce combat rising up in various areas.

Even fiercer was the fighting on the alliance's left flank.

Just outside the Gulf of Patras, where the bulk of the fighting was taking place, the sea was about forty or fifty meters deep. The area where Barbarigo was commanding the left flank, though, was only twenty to thirty meters deep, and immediately to the left of them the sea was less than fifteen meters deep. Go a little further and the depth suddenly went down to three meters and, closer to the shoals, down to one meter or less. The sea floor rose abruptly enough to take even the most experienced sailor by surprise.

Agostino Barbarigo had decided his strategy the previous night and was determined not to deviate from it. He planned to encircle the enemy ship on the right and then drive it into the shoals. The pirate Scirocco, however, was commanding the targeted vessel. If the Venetian captain knew these waters that well, surely the pirate captain who called them home did too. Scirocco was so notorious that even children all along the Mediterranean coastline knew his nickname. Barbarigo's plan would not be easy to execute.

Yet there was no other way to secure victory than by driving the enemy into the shoals. If the allies didn't do that to the Turks, the Turks would do it to the allies.

Barbarigo knew that he had no choice but to hit the enemy with all of his might regardless of the damage his ship or others in his formation might incur. They had to attack as a unified front. The pirates, even when supposedly fighting in the name of Islam, instinctively put the safety of their own ships first. The Venetians, on the other hand, fought with the interests of the Republic at the forefront of their minds.

The two galleasses in Barbarigo's left flank had begun firing with the others and had thrown the Turkish right flank into disarray. Even in these perilous waters, however, it hadn't taken the Turkish fleet long to recover from the initial setback. The right flank passed by both sides of the two galleasses and raced at top speed toward the advancing allied fleet. Quirini, though, followed Barbarigo's plan and allowed the Turkish ships to slip past as he turned to the right. The entire left flank of the allied fleet followed suit.

The allied ships executed their strategy flawlessly. As the enemy's attention was naturally focused on Barbarigo's crimson-painted flagship, which held steady, Quirini's ship managed to turn behind the enemy's fleet in an instant. The allied left flank, stringed between

Quirini and Barbarigo's ships, now surrounded the crescent of the Turkish right. The next step was to tighten the ring.

Forcing the enemy ships into the shoals was all a matter of blocking off their movements. The Turkish right flank, however, consisted mainly of formidable pirate ships, so this could hardly be achieved from a safe distance. One's own freedom of movement had to be put at risk, but the three Venetian admirals, Barbarigo, Canale, and Quirini, never wavered.

The galleasses, now in a supporting role, provided cannon fire to assist the galleys in their close-quarter combat. The barrage coming from the far left galleass commanded by Ambrosio Bragadino was particularly intense and amply demonstrated the awesome power of the "floating batteries." Ambrosio was a relative of Marcantonio Bragadino, the commander on Cyprus who had been flayed alive. Ambrosio Bragadino had repositioned his massive ship faster than any of the other galleass captains and was showering the enemy's right flank with artillery fire.

The Turkish troops kept up determined resistance to the ever-tightening ring of the Venetian fleet, but the cannon barrage certainly must have dealt them both a physical and a psychological blow. The Turks simply were not as accustomed to cannon fire on the sea as they were on land. They watched masts being blown off and gaping holes being opened in the deck before their very eyes. They had no way of knowing when and from where the next cannon ball would strike. The allies could see the enemy begin to lose heart.

The cannons were not completely accurate, however, so the damage they inflicted was not limited to the Turkish side. As the Venetian ships further tightened their circle, cannon fire started hitting them as well. Bragadino was well aware of this, but continued firing regardless.

Barbarigo's crimson ship had held a position at the extreme left in the shallowest waters at which a galley could move, less than five meters deep. Suddenly, now, he headed directly for the center of the half circle, bringing Canale's ship along with him. They quickly connected their two ships with iron chains that were attached to the ships' sides. They rammed their prows into the Turkish ships, while the remaining ships of the left flank—also connected by chains—followed behind them.

Everywhere the oars of enemy and allied ships were tightly locked together. The ships lost all freedom of movement, creating gridlocked combat zones on the sea. If it was too far to leap, soldiers scrambled up and down the banks of locked oars onto the enemy ships. The Venetian oarsmen abandoned their oars and joined in the fray, clad in their customary breastplates and wielding clubs with a sharp iron stud at the end. Despite the chaos and confusion, the Christian soldiers were still easily distinguishable from the Muslims, who wore turbans of various colors and clutched crescent-shaped swords that gave off a dull glow.

At this point the battle was sheer hand-to-hand

combat. Barbarigo's vessel had knifed into the very center of the enemy flank, but he never took a step away from his post on the prow. He was encased in steel armor, his left hand wielding a drawn sword, his right signaling orders with a baton.

It suddenly occurred to him that his helmet might be preventing his voice from carrying, so he threw it on the deck. From the corner of his eye, he saw the commander of the ship to his right, Antonio da Canale, collapse. Canale's unique combat uniform—reminiscent of a polar bear—was entirely covered with enemy arrows. It was three o'clock in the afternoon.

Far from the hand-to-hand fighting in the shoals, an entirely different type of battle was unfolding on the right flank. Uluch Ali and Captain Doria were engaged in a battle of wits and technical acumen, a contest between two professionals at the top of their games.

One of those professionals, however, had made a miscalculation. Doria neglected to consider the pride of the Venetians who manned the 25 ships that made up nearly half of the 57-ship-strong right flank. The Venetians were also professionals, but their desire to put the interests of Venice first made them, in a sense, as ineffective as amateurs. Uluch Ali may have been leading a fleet of Turkish amateurs in addition to his own pirate ships, but at least the Turks followed his orders.

This battle took place in the open sea, where the water was about fifty meters deep and the northwest wind called the Mistral was blowing. Although it wasn't blowing terribly strongly, this wind favored Doria.

As previously noted, Doria moved his fleet far to the south at the beginning of the battle in an attempt to block Uluch Ali's mobility by circling to his right. Because of this, Doria's right flank didn't benefit from the artillery support from the galleasses enjoyed by the left flank and the main force. The lumbering galleasses couldn't keep up with Doria's sudden change in tactics and thus simply remained in their predetermined locations, turning their attention to the enemy's main force instead. In other words, Uluch Ali's fleet didn't sustain much damage at all from the galleass bombardment.

Doria, seeing that Ali's ships were virtually unharmed, moved his own ship even farther south. This unplanned maneuver caused the distances between the ships in his formation to grow that much wider. It was only when the allied battle line had been stretched too thin to be able to return to its original configuration that Doria realized Uluch Ali's strategy presented him with a new and unexpected twist.

In fact, all of this had been Uluch Ali's plan from the very beginning. He intended first to go around the left side of Doria's fleet and then to strike Don Juan's main fleet from behind. Doria had sensed this and moved his ships to prevent him from outflanking him. Uluch Ali wasn't foolish enough to face Doria's fleet head-on, quickly and skillfully turning the prow of his ship towards the northwest. Doria's movement towards the south had opened up a gap between his fleet and Don Juan's main force. Uluch Ali now focused on this gap, which presented an opening for him to attack Don Juan's fleet from the rear—his intention all along.

The Venetians in the right flank immediately saw through Uluch Ali's plan. They had been following Doria's ship but had stopped once Doria started heading too far south. Seeing Uluch Ali's fleet pass right before their eyes, the 25 or so Venetian ships rushed en masse to attack, but not because they had been given any such order. The Venetians had reacted as if by reflex.

The Turks' left flank led by Uluch Ali consisted of 94 ships, including the small ones. Although the Venetians attacked only one section of the Turkish line, they suddenly found themselves fighting five or six enemy ships apiece.

It was a massacre. The Turkish boats were like schools of piranha feeding on the flesh of much larger fish; the dying fish could possibly kill a few piranha before expiring, but the killers just kept coming in wave after wave.

Benedetto Solanzo, the captain of one of those Venetian ships, watched as the majority of his crew was killed. When he saw six Turkish crafts surround his ship as if to suck out the last drops of its blood, he ordered the few remaining oarsmen to jump into the sea. He then went down into the hold of his ship and lit the gunpowder, blowing himself up along with the six surrounding enemy ships. His remains were never found.

The damage to the Venetian forces was severe. The number of ship's captains who died in battle on the right flank rivaled the number on the left flank, which engaged in hand-to-hand combat.

As the ships in his fleet routed the Venetians and Doria struggled to change direction, Uluch Ali succeeded in reaching the rightmost portion of Don Juan's main fleet. His seamanship was astonishing indeed.

Lepanto – October 7, 1571 – Evening

Even at sea, a "battleground" of sorts was formed when war galleys locked oars. Hand-to-hand combat became the only possible way of engaging the enemy, which rendered the galleasses essentially ineffective. They could still knock down enemy masts with their cannons, but there was also a real possibility that the falling masts and yardarms would kill friendly forces fighting beneath them. The galleasses thus inevitably became mere observation posts after the middle stage of the battle. Francesco Duodo, the commander in charge of the six galleasses, gave the following official report when he returned to Venice after the battle:

"The Christians and the Muslims were like hunters in a forest. Though a lot was happening in other parts of the forest, the hunters remained focused on their own quarry, not paying any attention to what was happening elsewhere. This was the case at Lepanto, time and again."

The Janissaries, the backbone of the Turkish army, gave ample demonstration of their bravery as the fighting grew more chaotic and confused. These matchless warriors were assigned to the main force led by Ali Pasha. The Muslim flagships were concentrated within the Turkish main fleet, just as in the Christian fleet. Grand Admiral Ali Pasha's flagship was surrounded by large warships carrying the governors of various regions under Turkish rule. Needless to say, these ships were defended by elite soldiers from the Turkish army, most notably the

Janissaries. These warriors descended on the Christians like a fog.

Yet the warriors manning the flagships of Don Juan, Veniero, and Colonna at the center of the Christian fleet were no less courageous. Musket fire rang in their ears along with the eerie whistle of arrows slicing through the air. The Christian battle cries were indistinguishable from the enemy's. Even the Spanish knights, disoriented by the rolling of the seas, remained composed as they sought to steady their footing. Supreme Commander Don Juan and Lieutenant Supreme Commander Colonna, though certainly afforded the protection of these knights, made no move to retreat from their forward positions on their ships' bridges.

Veniero, for his part, stood completely unprotected on his ship's bridge. "The Fortress" was seventy-five-years old and his reflexes may have slowed, but he made the best of them. He used neither spear nor sword; when not shouting commands, he toppled enemy soldiers with the deadly accuracy of his crossbow. At his side were two attendants who handed him a freshly loaded crossbow whenever he released an arrow. He hadn't worn his helmet since the start of the battle, and his white hair blowing in the wind looked like the mane of a crazed horse. One arrow loosed by a faceless enemy lodged directly in his left thigh, but this did not topple "The Fortress." Veniero pulled it out with his own hands, mangled flesh still clinging to the tip, and tossed it aside as if it were nothing.

The Janissaries attacked Veniero's ship and, of course, Don Juan's. The Sardinian soldiers protecting the supreme commander's ship, however, carried out their duties valiantly. When they couldn't use guns, they attacked with swords. When they fell, fresh soldiers from the trailing ships replaced them. The Christian fleet's rear guard of thirty ships also joined in the fray. Two of the Venetian ships assigned to the rear guard moved forward when they noticed that Don Juan's vessel was in danger and, by doing so, managed to divert part of the Janissary attack. The soldiers of these two ships fought fiercely even after their captains had been killed.

The battle in the middle began to turn, if slightly, in the Christians' favor. Not only did the allies inflict significant damage on the Turkish fleet during the opening bombardment, but they also freed the Christian oarsmen aboard those ships that they captured. Those freed slaves then attacked the Muslims from behind.

The battle on the left flank, where Agostino Barbarigo was in command, was clearly turning in favor of the allied forces.

The enemy here were all pirates. If the Janissaries were the backbone of the Turkish army, then the Muslim pirates were the true strength of the Turkish navy and the equal of any battle-hardened warrior. That said, all but 12 of the 55 ships on the left flank were manned by Venetians; they had harbored a great deal of animosity for the Turks over the past few years. What was more, the

Turks had just taken Cyprus from them and had brutal-
ly massacred many compatriots in the process. Tactics
were not so much the issue here; more than weapons,
they wanted to use their bare hands, and even more than
their hands, they wanted to use the weight of their bodies to crush the Turkish foe.

But there was a steep price to pay. Antonio da
Canale, "The Wolf of the Cretan Sea," lay motionless at
the prow of his vessel, his white, quilted uniform stained
red. The ship's lieutenant had immediately taken
command after the captain had fallen in battle.

The greatest sacrifice borne on the front line of the
left flank was the loss of Admiral Barbarigo's flagship. It
was connected to Canale's by iron chains as part of his
plan to drive the enemy into the shoals. As they assault-
ed the enemy fleet, Barbarigo's ship attracted particular
attention from the enemy because his was the only one
painted crimson. Eight enemy craft surrounded and
attacked his ship. Even the masts and the yardarms were
on fire after the sails were set ablaze by the enemy's
flamed arrows. Most of its red oars had cracked and were
carried away by the waves.

Even then, not a single man abandoned ship. The
crew did their best to douse the flames, and everyone
who could wield a weapon—certainly the oarsmen, but
even the cook and the confessor priest—stood up against
the enemy soldiers. Here as well, they were able to occupy enemy ships and unbind the Christian slaves, who
then attacked the enemy from behind.

Barbarigo saw that the enemy was in trouble and realized that victory was at hand. He planted himself on the forward edge of the prow and did everything he could to spur his soldiers on.

At that moment, a musket shot struck his right eye. He felt as if his entire head had been struck with a piece of iron, and it was all he could do to remain upright. Scirocco's ship was slowly sinking into the muddy waters in front of him. He saw the wounded Scirocco jump into the sea only to be pulled out by a skiff manned by Venetian soldiers sent out to rescue allied survivors. Scirocco, pirate captain and governor of Alexandria, would die from his wounds three days later. Barbarigo only allowed himself to collapse once he had seen that the enemy captain had been taken out of action. Federico Nani, just a short distance away, immediately assumed command.

Barbarigo was carried below deck to the ship's hold. Had the stern not been so badly burned, he would have been carried to the captain's cabin on the bridge. The doctor was called. It turned out that Barbarigo was not just wounded in the right eye; an arrow had penetrated deep into one of the small seams in his armor. When the doctor pulled out the arrow, blood gushed out and covered the armor on the back of his legs, where it dried. Barbarigo had clearly lost a massive amount of blood, and fresh blood was still flowing out of his now shapeless right eye. Not even the doctor could stop it. Those present were astounded at how quickly his face was losing color.

Just then, a dispatch runner hurriedly descended the wooden stairs to give his report: all the ships in the enemy flank were sinking, burning, or captured, and the victory beacon had just been raised.

A calm smile spread for the first time across Agostino Barbarigo's pale face.

The main force sent up their beacon at almost exactly the same time as the left flank.

The fierce fighting had finally died down. Ali Pasha's defenseless flagship was brought before Don Juan for inspection. He found Ali Pasha's body lying in an elegant cabin situated on the stern, an arrow stuck deep in his heart. His two sons had been taken prisoner aboard their own ships.

The members of the alliance cut the head off the Turkish grand admiral's corpse, skewered it on a spear, and hoisted it atop the mast of Don Juan's flagship. As on Barbarigo's front, not a single Turkish ship escaped.

The battle between the Christian right flank and the Muslim left flank, on the other hand, was approaching a markedly different outcome. Doria and Uluch Ali were eyeing each other warily from a safe distance. Although their two ships were leading their respective battle lines, they never engaged each other directly.

Since Doria had only been stalking the enemy without actually attacking, the Venetian ships under his command had decided to revolt and engage Uluch Ali's

Galley (Turkish)

fleet on their own. This act had been doomed to end in a heroic struggle that culminated in Benedetto Solanzo's suicide bombing. Six of the twenty-five Venetian captains in the right flank died in battle, the same ratio as that of Barbarigo's left flank. While these waters thus saw their share of fierce battle, the overall maneuvering was reminiscent of Nelson at the Battle of Trafalgar many years later, or even of Heihachiro Togo at the Battle of the Japan Sea in the twentieth century. One could say that this battle saw the birth of modern naval warfare.

Uluch Ali's left flank attacked the Venetian fleet where it could and dodged it where it couldn't. The Turks managed to make it to waters where Doria could not chase them down even if he wanted to, and proceeded to home in on Don Juan's main force.

Three ships belonging to the Knights of the Order of St. John from Malta guarded the right edge of the main fleet. The leader of the Knights sailed in the flagship to the far right, which carried numerous French and Spanish knights whose lives were consecrated to God and to combating the infidel. The children of a great number of Europe's aristocratic families belonged to this order.

For the Muslim pirate Uluch Ali, a former Christian, there was no target that he wanted to attack more than these ships. He was, furthermore, the governor of Algiers. This encounter between the pirate headquartered in Algiers and the knights who had fortified the island of Malta seemed like a fateful one indeed.

Uluch Ali launched a fierce attack on the Maltese ships from behind while these were busy with the battle raging between the main fleets. The knights on the Maltese flagship fought valiantly, but in the end those who fell were not the turbaned, scimitar-wielding Muslim pirates, but rather the elegant figures clad in armor. Uluch Ali first confiscated the Knights' flag. He then seized the flagship itself, even as the knights and their leader were still aboard fighting.

But Uluch Ali was not a hunter in the forest; he was one of a dwindling number of Ottoman warriors. He couldn't overlook the victory signals, first from the left flank, and then from the main force. The pirate changed his ship's direction once again. He turned a hundred and eighty degrees around towards Doria, this time with the

Maltese flagship in tow.

Uluch Ali clearly intended to flee, but this was something that the Venetian ships under Doria's command, once again, did not miss. Those vessels that hadn't been sunk united in an attack on the Turkish left flank, whose hulls were passing by in front of them.

At this point, the ships of other states besides Venice also decided they couldn't sit idly by. Ships from Florence and Savoy spearheaded the assault into the battle line. Indeed, Captain Doria could not simply sit back, either, as the flagship of Malta was being towed away. All the ships in the allied right flank joined in the attack, and within moments they were destroying one Turkish ship after another. The Maltese flagship was set free, but the flag of the order remained in the hands of the pirates.

The allied right flank had finally launched a unified attack. Uluch Ali nonetheless escaped, albeit with only four ships. He reached the Turkish capital of Constantinople along with twenty-seven ships that had been left behind at Modone on the southern tip of the Peloponnesian peninsula. One can only pity the galley slaves on these ships, who had to continue rowing under the whip even after seeing their compatriots set free practically before their eyes.

Sailing into the harbor of the Golden Horn after a journey of more than forty days, Uluch Ali's ship dragged in the water behind it the flag of the Knights of St. John.

The waters of Lepanto were filled with the corpses of both allied and enemy warriors. The burning ships scattered about marked the areas where the fighting had been the fiercest. The only bodies moving between the listing ships were Turkish soldiers desperately swimming in an attempt to stay alive.

So much blood had been spilled that the deep blue sea now looked as if it had been mixed with red wine. Little by little, the setting sun in the west turned those seas a golden hue. It seemed the victors had forgotten to raise a cheer of triumph. Over the sea where the naval battle of the century had just ended, an eerie silence reigned.

Lepanto – October 7, 1571 – Night

Slowly but surely dusk descended upon the sea. The winds began to blow harder and the waves grew in size. No one could have predicted that nightfall would bring such a dramatic change in the climate. If the weather got any worse it would become dangerous to stay at sea.

There was a small island called Petras six nautical miles to the northeast. Though near the Greek mainland, the island was not under Turkish control. The allied fleet could at least spend the night in Petras's harbor. They towed along all of the enemy ships that still seemed seaworthy. They left the badly burned corpses and ships to the waves.

When they arrived at Petras, all the commanders assembled on Don Juan's ship to congratulate one another. The twenty-six-year-old supreme commander, excited at having attained his first great victory, immediately rushed to embrace Veniero, who appeared vigorous despite his bloodstained bandages. Don Juan was so concerned about Veniero that he had forgotten his superior rank. The old Venetian admiral responded warmly, as if he were celebrating the victory with his own son. Colonna entered, leading the nephew of Pope Pius V and the other Roman aristocracy. The narrow cabin filled with loud, laudatory greetings.

When Doria entered the room, however, the joyousness faded as if stifled by a mass of cold air. Everyone stared at his armor, noticeable for not being stained with a single drop of the enemy's blood. Don Juan and Colonna's uniforms were stained with splattered blood in several places, and Veniero's body was practically covered in it.

Doria approached Don Juan and congratulated him on the victory in a calm voice as if he himself had not been involved. The supreme commander gave a curt and chilly response. The Venetian admirals looked at the Genoese sea captain with barely suppressed fury. Everybody by this point knew the pertinent facts of Doria's actions on the right flank and their consequences. When Pope Pius V later heard the report, he made a remark that no doubt expressed the feelings of the victorious troupe at that moment: "O Lord, have mercy upon this pitiful man who behaved like a pirate rather than a sea captain!"

Doria might have considered this criticism overly harsh, but the Battle of Lepanto was in the end a battle between galleys, not a contest between sailing vessels such as at Trafalgar.

At any rate, the joy of the victors knew no bounds. They had proven that the Turkish military, once thought to be invincible, could be overcome. The powers of Christendom had repeatedly faced Turkish offensives since the fall of Constantinople in 1453 but had rarely put up any solid opposition. This was actually the first real victory against the Turks in the 118 years since then—even though Uluch Ali had gotten away, it could well be called a total victory.

Young Don Juan was in a mood to share his joy with everybody. While he had greeted Doria in a less than warm manner, he uttered no words of recrimination, either. Now, the face of the one man who was absent from that night's celebration, a face that had always been present at the leaders' council, came to the young prince's mind. Accompanied only by Colonna and Veniero, he exited the cabin and ordered a skiff to come pick them up.

The men on the surrounding ships immediately noticed the supreme commander standing on the deck with his two deputies and let out a wild cheer. Knights, crossbowmen, gunners, sailors and oarsmen all joined in. The slaves freed from Muslim ships, and former convicts who would be free men from this day, cheered especially loudly. With no enemy to worry about that night, they burned their torches brightly, illuminating the great fleet and the small harbor so that it almost appeared to be daytime.

The skiff carrying the troika of commanders pulled up alongside Barbarigo's flagship. Badly damaged, it could no longer sail by itself and had been towed into the harbor. The crimson masts were broken in half, the yardarms had burned down, and more than half of the oars were missing. The three admirals boarded the ship and went below deck to the hold where Barbarigo lay.

Veniero had been informed of his adjutant's serious injuries just as the battle was coming to an end and had sped to Barbarigo's ship right away. Quirini, the admiral who had fought alongside Barbarigo, was already at his side when Veneiro arrived. Although they had come at once, the two Venetian commanders had been informed by the doctor that Barbarigo, looking deathly pale, was already beyond help.

Don Juan was thus aware of the seriousness of Barbarigo's condition before he visited his bedside. Neither the young prince nor Colonna were able to offer any words of comfort. When Barbarigo recognized the supreme commander, he tried to raise himself off the bed but didn't have the strength. Don Juan knelt down beside him and lightly placed his hand over Barbarigo's icy right hand. In a whispered mixture of Italian and Spanish, he told Barbarigo of the allied fleet's triumph.

Don Juan had had a favorable impression of Barbarigo ever since their first meeting in Messina. Even when he and Veniero had been at each other's necks, Don Juan had always been happy to see Barbarigo; the latter's calm and unobtrusive manner, firm resolve, and consistency had inspired the young man's respect and admiration. Barbarigo was the sole casualty among the allied fleet's high command, and the prince's heart was filled with grief for him.

Barbarigo could only answer the supreme commander's kind words with a weak smile. Don Juan, now gripping his hand with both of his own, stood up. Quirini then led him and Colonna out of the ship's hold, Veniero alone remaining behind.

The seventy-five-year-old commander stood in the same spot previously occupied by Don Juan. He attempted to kneel but found it impossible to bend his knee because of the wound to his leg. True to his nature, he would die before expressing a word of comfort. Instead, he bluntly said, "If there's anything you need me to do, don't hesitate to ask."

Barbarigo immediately thought of Flora. At first he imagined her resting her head on his right arm as she always did. Then memories came flooding back of her surrendering herself to him completely, arms wrapped around his neck.

He began retracing the past. The memory of the square in front of the Church of San Zaccaria where he had first met her was as vibrant as if it had happened yesterday. He recalled the boy following his mother around like a puppy, chatting away, and her gentle, patient answers to his questions.

The smile that now appeared on Barbarigo's face came from the bottom of his heart. As long as she had her son, Flora could go on living. And she would know that even after death—especially after death—he would be by her side, protecting them. The two sources of support would allow her to go on.

Barbarigo couldn't ask Veniero, who hated any kind of impropriety, to look after the mother and child, so he simply looked up at Veniero and slowly shook his head. The veteran admiral, after staring at Barbarigo for a moment longer, left the hold of the ship. Barbarigo was alone.

He no longer felt any pain. An overwhelming urge to sleep washed over him. Although he tried again to summon her image, what had seemed so fresh in his mind just moments ago refused to revive. Then suddenly, quite suddenly, he felt her in his hands, as if he were caressing her long hair, her soft, full hair, and touching her cool forehead and the slender nape of her neck. And then he saw her, smiling through her tears, and felt those tears against his fingertips as he wiped them away.

The Venetian commander had already breathed his last when the servants entered the hold. In the "Record of the Battle of Lepanto" prepared by the government of the Venetian Republic, the following line was dedicated to him: "*Provveditore Generale* Agostino Barbarigo was welcomed into the ranks of the most blessed through the kind of death that he had hoped for."

The Island of Corfu – Autumn 1571

When the members of the allied fleet pulled into the Venetian outpost of Corfu, they began to assess the results of the battle. They had captured 117 enemy galleys and 110 smaller vessels. All other enemy ships had either sunk or burned during the battle, excluding the four with which Uluch Ali had escaped.

The Islamic side suffered approximately 8,000 deaths in the battle. Among them were the top commanders: Ali Pasha; the captain of the Janissaries; the governors of Lesbos, Chios, Negroponte, and Rhodes. Two sons of Barbarosa, the famous pirate from a generation earlier, were also among the casualties. Nearly all of the key members of the Turkish fleet had perished in the battle.

The allies took approximately 10,000 prisoners, among them the two sons of Ali Pasha. Don Juan chose them as gifts to present to the Spanish king. The pirate Scirocco had also been among the prisoners, but died two days after the battle. Many ministers of the Turkish court were also taken prisoner. Nearly 15,000 Christian slaves were set free.

The spoils of war were divided among the allied participants according to the resources supplied to the war effort. The Spanish king received 57 war galleys and a commensurate number of prisoners. Most of the gold and other valuables found on board those ships would also become possessions of the king, with Don Juan taking the rest.

The Republic of Venice received 43 galleys, 39 large cannons and 86 smaller cannons. In addition, it received 1,162 prisoners, two of whom were given personally to Veniero.

The Papal States, the Order of the Knights of St. John, the Duchy of Savoy, and all other participating forces were not neglected in the division of the spoils. The Papal States had not previously owned a single warship but now owned seventeen. They were also given 541 of the prisoners.

At the same time, nobody could call the sacrifices made by the Christian side insignificant. The death toll was only a few hundred less than the Islamic side: 7,500 men. There were approximately 8,000 wounded, including the young Miguel de Cervantes, who had fought aboard a ship assigned to the left flank and taken a gunshot to his left arm. The following table shows the numbers of wounded and dead among the main participating countries:

	Dead	Wounded
Spain	2000	2200
Papal States	800	1000
Venice	4836	4584

Only Venice's numbers are exact because only Venice valued accurate statistics. Spain and the Papal States hadn't kept close count even as the soldiers had first boarded their ships. If a man didn't answer during roll call, he was considered one of the dead.

Given the ratio of personnel that the Venetians had contributed, their fatality rates were inordinately high. The number of Venetian commanders who died in battle is particularly striking. Other than two members of the Orsini family aboard the flagship of the Papal States, nearly all of the high-ranking commanders who died in battle were Venetians.

All of the eighteen ship captains who were killed were Venetian. The Barbarigo family lost four men, including three ship's captains, and the Contarini family lost two. There was also one victim each in the Solanzo and Veniero families, both of them ship's captains. Names from the most exalted of the noble families who colored the thousand-year history of Venice fill the registers of the Lepanto dead. The Venetian Republic, as precise as ever in their accounting, sub-divided the list of casualties by specialty:

	Dead	Wounded
Captains (noble)	12	5
Captains (citizen)	6	20
Troop commanders	5	20
Scribes (lieutenant's rank)	6	4
Master sailors	7	10
Sailors	124	118
Artillerymen	113	79
Carpenter's mates	32	78

Confessor priests	5	3
Lead oarsmen	921	681
Oarsmen	2272	2479
Soldiers	1333	1087
Total	4836	4584

It was not only the aristocracy who fought with everything they had. The figures suggest everyone on the Venetians ships, down to the cooks, took part in the fighting.

The dead, excluding those who disappeared in the waves, were interred on Corfu. Few of the non-Venetian dead were repatriated, either. The beautiful island of Corfu became their final resting place.

Their graves can be found on a hillside that faces east and is bathed in sunlight during the day. The vast cemetery came to be called "The Tomb of the Warriors of Lepanto" and that was its name for two centuries.

Venice – Autumn 1571

The night they arrived in Corfu, Veniero immediately dispatched a high-speed ship to report the news of the victory. When the ship reached Venice, the Turkish battle flag dragging in the sea behind it, great excitement broke out among the Venetian citizenry.

Everyone knew how great the sacrifice had been, but even for those bereaved by the loss of a family member, this battle was different. Venice had swallowed defeat after defeat for over a hundred years against the Turks. The sailors from other countries could run away when they saw the Turkish crescent on the horizon, but the Venetians had been the great power of the Mediterranean and had no choice but to worry about the Turks every hour of the day. Those Turks had been thoroughly trounced.

The Venetians, generally known for their temperate personalities, were in a frenzy of jubilation. House lamps burned deep into the night, while excited crowds filled the public squares. Taverns greeted the dawn with their doors wide open.

Government officials shed tears of joy when they received the news of the victory, but they were also concerned about the safety of the Turkish and Arab traders living in the city. The government confined all of the Muslims in Venice to a single residence within the city to protect them from possible attacks by citizens overly intoxicated with victory. This led to the foundation of the Turkish Trading House.

The government also declared October 7th a state holiday that would be celebrated every year to commemorate this highly unusual victory. It also commissioned Titian, the greatest painter of the republic, to work on a great mural depicting the battle. Titian declined, however, because King Philip II of Spain had already commissioned him for a painting of the same subject. He had turned eighty-three that year; not only was he the greatest painter in Venice; he was considered the best in all of Europe. In the final analysis, it was the Spanish king and not the Venetian government that served as Titian's patron and paid his pension. The Venetians realized this and had no choice but to commission the work with someone else.

Finding that someone else was not difficult. Titian's replacement was Tintoretto, fifty-three-years old and in his prime. Indeed, when it came to large works, Tintoretto's technique was superior to Titian's. Tintoretto began the work immediately.

His grand painting, which, supposedly, even depicted the moment when Agostino Barbarigo received his mortal wound, was completed three years later in 1574 and adorned a room of the Palazzo Ducale. Unfortunately, it was destroyed by fire in 1577. A mural depicting the same subject that was painted years after the fire by Andrea Vicentino can be found today in the *Sala dello Scrutinio* or voting chamber of the Palazzo Ducale. Veniero is shown near the center of this large painting, but Barbarigo does not appear.

Nonetheless, as joyful was that autumn of 1571, no splendid celebration was held in Venice to greet the triumphant admirals. They may have won the Battle of Lepanto, but the Venetian Republic continued to face unresolved problems.

Grecian Waters – Winter 1571

Veniero wanted to return east immediately. The Mediterranean was now practically wide open. The Turkish navy had been decimated and many of the pirate captains had found a watery grave in the waters of Lepanto. The Venetians could now reclaim the bases along the Peloponnesian peninsula that had been stolen by the Turks. They could also perhaps recover the recently lost Cyprus, the occupation of which was not yet complete. While in Corfu, Veniero had tirelessly advocated this course of action to Don Juan.

The young supreme commander, however, was drunk with the glorious victory that had become his. The fact that it had not been the result of years of careful planning but had virtually fallen into his lap made it even more intoxicating. His strength, or what perhaps should be called his will, contributed decisively to winning at Lepanto, but the young prince was no longer able to think objectively, to consider, coolly, how this might be extended into further victories. The ministers to the Spanish king kept emphasizing that it was no longer the appropriate season for sailing. Colonna, who was imagining the prizes he would receive from Pius V as soon as he returned to Rome, was also not of a mind to set out to sea again.

Veniero was alone. With every passing day, Don Juan seemed to forget the camaraderie they had shared immediately following the battle. Not only that, he was outraged that Veniero had dispatched a ship carrying the news of the victory to Venice without first asking his permission. Yet again, relations between the Spanish and Italian commanders grew strained. Furthermore, Barbarigo was no longer present to represent Venice's interests while appeasing Don Juan and Colonna.

For the time being, the allies decided to rendezvous the following spring, 1572. They would meet on Corfu instead of Messina.

Once this much was decided, Don Juan took his fleet and sailed west. Colonna also took his share of the captured ships and headed toward Ancona, a port on the Adriatic Sea controlled by the Papal States. He would go by land from Ancona to Rome, where a lavish spectacle in his honor hosted by the Pope would be waiting. The ships of the other states also departed for home, as did Doria.

The Venetian fleet alone remained in Corfu. It would have been impossible for the Venetians to set out alone on an expedition into the Eastern Mediterranean. It was all they could do to defend Corfu, the linchpin of the Adriatic Sea, and Crete, the Venetian staging point in the Aegean. Furthermore, the allied fleet was scheduled to meet in Corfu the spring after. The fact that the entire Venetian fleet decided to remain at the rendezvous point a half year in advance is the ultimate proof of Venice's expectation that another allied fleet would be formed.

Don Juan returned to Messina on November 1st. The southern island of Sicily, property of the Spanish king, was where the fleet would spend the winter and revel in the glory of victory.

Several weeks later, Sebastiano Veniero headed back to Venice alone, but not in order to attend a victory tribute. He had been officially recalled by the Venetian government.

Constantinople – Winter 1571

The Venetian ambassador Barbaro remained in Constantinople with his windows boarded up. Although he passed even the day by candlelight, he never tired of gathering information to send back to his homeland. He had heard news of Uluch Ali's return with 31 ships on the eighteenth of November, one month and ten days after the Battle of Lepanto. He accurately guessed that only four of those 31 ships had actually survived the Battle of Lepanto. As usual, he secretly sent this information in code back to the Venetian homeland.

Several days later, Ambassador Barbaro breathed fresh air once again for the first time in a year and a half. He had received a summons from Grand Vizier Sokullu. Unlike his prior communications with the grand vizier, which had been sent through the Jewish physician, this was an invitation to an official meeting. Following convention, Ambassador Barbaro dressed formally and departed the embassy with three assistants and one interpreter.

The ambassador, who was in his sixties, thought that getting used to riding on horseback again over the steep hills of Pera would take a lot of effort. When as they rode down the slope toward the Golden Horn, the ambassador's boat, which had been long unused, was there waiting for them. They boarded, crossed the Golden Horn, and arrived at Constantinople proper on the opposite shore. A short, gentle climb from there and

a left turn led them through the central gate of the Topkapi Palace.

Barbaro had heard about the waning fortunes of the
neighborhoods along the Golden Horn, but seeing it
with his own eyes after more than a year away was a different matter. Though trade was never the Turks' strong
suit, the decline seemed quite extraordinary. While the
activities of the empire's Greek and Jewish subjects were
of some help, the total disruption of trade with Western
Europe made the ensuing economic deterioration impossible to cover up. With the capital in such a condition,
one could only imagine the state of affairs in Syria or
Egypt. Even on Rhodes, now ruled by the Turks, the
island's past prosperity was only a memory—no doubt
that the future of Cyprus held something similar in
store.

In other words, Western European traders weren't
the only ones taking a hit. The Turks were also losing
ground, though that certainly didn't hinder their desire
for territorial expansion. The thought of it all was
enough to drive Barbaro, who was responsible for protecting Venice's interests, to a kind of mute despair.

After entering Topkapi Palace's central gate, he
passed through a large courtyard crossed by a number of
wide roads. To his right was the vast commissary that fed
the sultan's entire court. To the left were the guards'
quarters. If one continued along the center road, one
would reach a second gate. Within that gate were the

libraries and reception halls, that is to say, the sultan's public and ceremonial spaces.

The smaller road on the far left took one to the harem, the private space where the sultan lived with his wives and concubines. No man, not even a member of the kitchen staff, could enter those precincts. It was a world where the sultan was the sole man, surrounded by large numbers of women and children, though there were some eunuchs as well.

People serving in the Turkish court and ambassadors and foreign dignitaries were all very familiar with the path that ran between the path to the harem and the center road. This was because the cabinet meetings were held in a chamber at the end of this path, right behind the sultan's private quarters.

Barbaro went down that path. Normally this great garden was literally buried in green, but now at the end of November it looked quite desolate. The garden itself was well tended, but nothing could be done about the withered leaves strewn along the path in scattered piles.

Yet Ambassador Barbaro's heart was dancing amidst this wintry desolation. Even for a veteran diplomat such as himself, the victory at Lepanto was too magnificent an event for him not to feel elated.

Grand Vizier Sokullu was waiting in the cabinet chamber with the junior viziers to his left and right. Barbaro recognized the face of Piali Pasha, well known as an anti-European hardliner.

In the past, even ambassadors representing sovereign states had been required to prostrate themselves in the manner of vassals while at the Ottoman court. This was still expected during an audience with the sultan. For Western Europeans, however, this manner of bowing was considered humiliating. The major powers of Spain, France, Venice, and the kingdom of the German Hapsburgs had been exempted from this practice since the time of the previous sovereign, the magnanimous Sultan Suleiman. For a conference with the grand vizier or the other viziers, there was no need to bow as if before the sultan. Moreover, a seat would be provided.

It was the Turkish fashion to sit cross-legged on chairs that were not only broad and comfortable, but also relatively low. The modern-day sofa or couch, built for comfort with various types of padding and covered with a variety of fabrics, is actually just an improvement on this Turkish-style divan.

Indeed, the practice of referring to the cabinet chamber in the Turkish palace as the "divan" came from the couches lining that chamber. There is a hotel in present-day Istanbul named Divan, and it is meant to evoke the idea of a ministerial cabinet rather than a humble couch. In contemporary Italian, a couch is still called a *divano*, and the word "sofa" is of similar origin. The original root of the word "divan" is either Arabic or Persian.

This type of couch did not start to become popular in Western Europe until after the seventeenth century, and it was not until the Rococo period in the eighteenth century that the most elegant ones were made. No such couches were made in Western Europe prior to the sixteenth century; all were imported from the Orient. The closest thing to a Renaissance-period couch would be something like a long, wooden trunk.

The ambassador was seated, not in the Turkish fashion, but on a soft chair in Western European style. He had the uncanny feeling that somebody was standing behind him to the right. His assistants were waiting outside the chamber and his interpreter was behind him to the left. The viziers were standing on his left. There shouldn't have been anyone behind him to the right.

He was not mistaken. Part of the wall on that side was inlaid with marble fretwork and beyond that hung a thick curtain. His sense that another person was in the room came from behind that curtain.

Barbaro had heard rumors that the sultan had specially ordered the construction of a window in order to secretly observe his viziers. The presence he sensed must have been that of Sultan Selim standing at that window. Selim, unlike his father Suleiman, had delegated all responsibilities of governance to his viziers because he preferred to spend his time with his harem. At the same time, however, he had devised this cunning method of keeping an eye on them.

The mood in the room made clear to Barbaro that he wasn't going to like what he was about to hear. Even if he appealed to principles of mutual self-interest, there was nobody here with whom he could find common ground. The reasonable discussions he had once had with the grand vizier were now a thing of the past.

As expected, the grand vizier began speaking to him in a very cold tone. "In the naval battle in the seas off Lepanto, we clearly suffered a crushing defeat. We have succeeded, however, in taking Cyprus. In other words, you have lost an arm, while we have lost our beard. The beard will grow back, while the arm cannot be regained."

To his great chagrin, the Venetian ambassador had to admit to himself the absolute truth of the grand vizier's words. At the same time, though, he couldn't help noticing that the old vizier's eyes were intently focused on him, as if trying to ask something. Barbaro couldn't forget his responsibilities as his country's representative; he ignored the grand vizier's unspoken signal, revealing no expression whatsoever. Instead he stressed just how important the results of the battle were, and predicted with optimism that the Western European alliance would hold up indefinitely. The hardliner Piali Pasha's face grew bright red with rage.

With this, the audience ended. Once again, Barbaro was sent to the boarded-up embassy, where he would take up his pen to write the day's events in a two-part report to his home government. He wrote the first part in standard script in the Venetian dialect, but for the second part he used code. In the coded report, Barbaro mentioned the grand vizier's meaningful look and his own opinion of what that look had meant.

The Venetian Council of Ten, however, did not respond with an order to reopen peace negotiations with the Ottoman Empire. In 1572, Venice was willing to stake everything on the continued existence of the alliance.

Though he didn't receive any directives from home, Ambassador Barbaro was still able to keep himself occupied.

Sultan Selim apparently didn't blame Uluch Ali for running home; he even gave the former Christian pirate a new nickname, "Kilic Ali." This caught the old ambassador's attention: "Kilic Ali" in Turkish means "Ali the Sword." The sultan appointed "Ali the Sword" to be the new grand admiral of the Turkish navy and ordered him to oversee the rebuilding of the Islamic fleet.

Uluch Ali took full advantage of the fact that winter discouraged sea travel. While the Christian ships were idling in their southern ports, he alone was active. The shipbuilding centers in Constantinople and Gallipoli worked at full capacity to turn out ships. The sultan had promised him unlimited resources.

The results were startling. On January 5, 1572, less than three months after the defeat at Lepanto, the scale of the rebuilding was reported to the sultan as follows:

Galleys launched	45
Galleys completed	25
Galleys nearly completed	11

Galleys in early stages	8
Small galleys launched	8

Besides these, 102 ships were under construction in harbors throughout Asia Minor and Greece. This made for a total of 199 ships, a navy rivaling the one that entered the Battle of Lepanto.

The massive fleet would set out into the Mediterranean once spring arrived, and Uluch Ali would be in command. Barbaro's pen scratched out a sad tune as it recorded these dire facts. Venice would once again have to confront an indomitable adversary.

In the Islamic world, a beard is the ultimate sign of manhood. The only males who didn't wear beards were those too young to grow them, or homosexuals. The Turkish military, shorn of its beard at Lepanto, had reemerged in full masculine adulthood within the space of half a year.

Meanwhile, in Western Europe, the sixty-eight-year-old Pope Pius V's health was getting precarious.

Rome – Spring 1572

Compared to the negotiations in 1571, when the members of the alliance were trying to gauge one another's true intentions while also feeling resigned to the fact that they had simply come too far to turn back, the negotiations of 1572 were bound to go smoothly.

All present agreed that if they exploited the momentum of their victory at Lepanto and kept pursuing the now weakened Turks, their triumph would be complete. The Kingdom of Spain, the Republic of Venice and the Papal States—the main forces in the Allied Fleet of the Holy League—were indeed very pleased with the remarkable results of the previous year's battle. The Papal States no longer even seemed concerned about bringing the English, the French, or even the German princes into the fold. The Pope's special envoys didn't have to go galloping on horseback over the muddy roads of Northern Europe that spring.

There was also no debate about who would be supreme commander; no one wanted to replace Don Juan. Even the Venetians acknowledged the young leader's special flair for leading an international alliance of this kind. There were also no objections to Marcantonio Colonna as the lieutenant supreme commander.

Even the problem of how to parcel out the expenses was resolved from the outset. The captured Turkish ships and prisoners had been divided to the participating states' satisfaction, heading off any repeat of the previous year's contentious arguments over piddling details. Every alliance member hoped to contribute as many ships and men as it could. In fact, even the minor powers such as Savoy and the Knights of St. John had quickly repaired the Turkish ships they had won. There was thus no need to build new ships, which was fortunate since there wasn't enough time to do so. Possessing no fleet of their own in 1571, the Papal States had to grant the Grand Duke Medici of Tuscany official recognition of his title of grand duke in exchange for ships. Now, however, with seventeen vessels, the Papal States were something of a naval power.

The Venetian Republic no longer had the trouble providing troops that it had the year before thanks to an outbreak of disease and the pinning down of five thousand recruits at the home port. Those five thousand were still available, and, in addition, the republic now had over one thousand Turkish prisoners who could be used as oarsmen, an advantage previously unavailable to them.

Using chained slaves as oarsmen did have its benefits. Sea captains in those times claimed the best oarsmen were the Dalmatians or the Greeks, but next came slaves, who were easier to use than Northern Italian volunteers with no maritime experience. The following table shows the origins of the oarsmen in the Venetian fleet just before the Battle of Lepanto.

War Galleys
    Volunteers from the Venetian Homeland   38 ships

Venetian Convicts	16 ships
Volunteers from Crete	30 ships
Volunteers from Venetian Colonies in the Ionian	7 ships
Volunteers from Dalmatian Territory	8 ships
Volunteers from Northern Italian Provinces	5 ships
Galleasses	
Volunteers from the Venetian Homeland	6 ships
Total	110 ships

Since volunteers were freemen, they had to be paid a salary. Such expenses were not a concern with convicts or slaves. Despite the savings, however, the Venetian Republic simply couldn't entrust the oars of all its ships to slaves.

It was a characteristic of Venetian ships that the oarsmen were seated on deck. The exception was the galleass, a likely target of cannon fire. Since galley warfare usually consisted of close fighting, even the oarsmen acted as soldiers and joined in the melee after there was no longer any need to maneuver the ship, a generations-old tradition in the Italian city-states, which were perennially short of manpower. Venice adhered to that tradition especially closely.

The armor that the oarsmen wore in those days—a kind of bullet- or arrow-proof vest—is still on display in the armaments room of the Palazzo Ducale in Venice. The vests were made from strong cloth and covered with iron studs. The oarsmen also wielded sharp, long poles covered with iron studs. There is evidence that Venice treated its oarsmen as full-fledged soldiers. If they fell in battle their families were provided with a pension, the same one denied to the families of aristocrats.

Venice not only treated its oarsmen well for hundreds of years, but also provided economic aid to the regions within its influence in return for the use of bases and port harbors. It was thus only natural that the residents of these regions came to be as loyal to the republic as the citizens of the Venice proper. Everybody in Dalmatia and on Corfu and other islands in the Ionian Sea did not doubt that their fates were entwined with that of the Republic of Venice. The uniquely loyal residents of these particular territories willingly aligned themselves with the Venetian Republic right up until its demise.

It is astonishing to see that the residents of Dalmatia, which is in the former Yugoslavia, are now so completely Slavic, while everything from their bell towers to their streets so closely resembles the Venetian style. The region was not only within the economic and military sphere of the republic, but also within its cultural sphere: replacing free oarsmen with Turkish slaves involved other issues besides the monetary savings. Besides which, slaves needed slave drivers, and such overseers were incompatible with the Venetian naval tradition.

Spain and the Papal States had encountered very few recruitment problems in 1571, and it seemed gathering men would be even easier in 1572.

The news of the victory at Lepanto had spread in a flash all along the Mediterranean coastline. Taking part in such a victory had given such men as who had signed up just to make a meager living a whole new outlook. Recruits came not only from the farming villages around Messina, Naples, and Genoa, but also from as far away as France and Germany. In no time there was a veritable flood of them.

These circumstances presented a golden opportunity. The government of Venice was united in its desire to make good use of it; they had to avoid repeating the mistake of having time for only one battle before the season for sailing was over. They had to make the most of the time they had, namely, the summer and half of the autumn. The allied fleet had to set sail as early as possible, even before summer began.

With that in mind, Venice decided to address all foreseeable problems in advance. First, Sebastiano Veniero was relieved of his position as commander in chief of the Venetian navy. Since it was not a question of dereliction of duty, he was not put on trial. The senate informed Veniero, who had been recalled to the homeland, that while there were no words of praise adequate to describe his heroics at the Battle of Lepanto, they thought he should step down for the best interests of the state. It was clear to them that Don Juan was not terribly fond of Veniero. The Venetian senate fired "The

Fortress" rather than offend the young royal. Foscarini, an admiral known for his affable personality, was given the post.

This was the worst blunder the Venetian government could have made. The Venetian fleet had lost Barbarigo and Canale. Venierio now retired, the only remaining admiral with combat experience was Marco Quirini.

But that wasn't the last of Venice's blunders. The government's approach to winning over Don Juan was also very poorly thought out. The Venetians though they could buy the skill and passion he had displayed at Lepanto by secretly promising to make him King of Morea.

Morea was the name for the Peloponnesian peninsula at that time. Venetian bases had been located at all of the peninsula's strategic points until the beginning of the sixteenth century. The two ports at the southern tip of the peninsula, Modone and Corone, were called the "The Two Eyes of Venice" and were the most vital bases after Crete, Cyprus, and Corfu. Even today, Venetian fortresses dot the harbors from those ports through Nafplion and even to Negroponte, capturing the eyes of all who enter. The Venetians were only slightly interested in controlling the interior, but were quite serious about securing the bases on the coastline.

Yet, beginning in the sixteenth century, the Turks, who had just destroyed the Byzantine Empire, began to take over the Peloponnesian peninsula little by little. Venice no longer had the power to stop them. First in the interior, then later in the coastal regions, Venetian out-posts turned into Turkish ones. This territory of "Morea" that the Venetians had promised Don Juan thus belonged almost entirely to the Turks; the Venetian promise was predicated on defeating the Turks and recovering all of it.

Promising to deliver territory that was in enemy hands might appear very foolish, but it was not an impossibility for Venice at that time, given a sufficient army. Don Juan was justifiably enthusiastic about the idea.

Although he was lauded as the hero of Lepanto, Don Juan was still outside the line of royal succession. It was not because his older brother Philip II had mustered brotherly affection for his dead father's bastard son that he finally recognized the prince, who was then fourteen. This was an age in which brothers who grew up together could easily turn into enemies; in fact, a brother was often a greater source of trouble than a stranger. Philip II thought of his half brother, seventeen years his junior, as only a pawn in a game. He might recognize him as the Duke of Austria, or even as a royal prince, but he didn't have the slightest inclination to allow him to become the king of anything.

Philip II was an able monarch, but not a man willing to open his heart. The unfortunate death of his son Don Carlos—an event that would later become famous through Verdi's opera of that name—conveys something dark about the tragic relationship between father and son for which the son was not wholly to blame. Philip had concealed his feelings even from his own son, so it was not surprising that he did not trust his half brother, especially one who was almost the same age as his son. The animosity between these two brothers, which had only been whispered of in the past, became an open topic of gossip after the Battle of Lepanto.

The Venetian government's actions only fueled the king's suspicions. Don Juan, furthermore, didn't have the strength of character to squarely face his powerful brother's suspicions and keep them at bay.

Though the "Crusade" of 1572 appeared at first glance to be progressing smoothly, it thus contained within it these seeds of discord.

Moreover, the passing of Pope Pius V on May 1st led to the election of Gregory XIII, an Italian like Pius V. The new Pope was a gentle man whose instinct was to avoid fighting.

Messina - Summer 1572

Venice already maintained a fleet of one hundred war galleys and six galleasses in Corfu, and preparations for the campaign were complete. The newly selected commander in chief of the Venetian navy, Foscarini, had been quick to arrive on the island.

Giovanni Solanzo, who had been selected to replace Barbarigo, set out in May from Corfu to Messina leading twenty-five galleys. He was going to rendezvous with the supreme commander of the allied fleet, Don Juan, who was already waiting there. There was also word that Colonna, leading the fleet of the Papal States, was on his way south. The commander of the Spanish fleet, Marquis de Santa Cruz, had left the assembly point in Naples with thirty-six ships. Two ships were also heading north from Malta.

After the Venetian admiral arrived in Messina, however, an unforeseen problem arose. Like the year before, the Spanish ministers accompanying Don Juan once again began making unbending demands about where the campaign should take place. They insisted that this year's fleet should go to North Africa to attack the pirates. The Venetians wanted to go east, like the year before, to destroy the Turkish fleet. They had received word that a Turkish armada led by Uluch Ali had left Constantinople.

The Spaniards refused to back down and the conflict only intensified. Meanwhile, Colonna came into port. Marquis de Santa Cruz also arrived, but that only put another vote in the Spanish column.

Don Juan finally took responsibility for presenting some kind of compromise. He proposed to Philip II that they first cooperate with the Venetians on a Cypriot campaign in exchange for the acquisition of new territory in the Eastern Mediterranean. No reply came from Madrid. Don Juan then proposed for the Spanish fleet to attack Algiers alone that summer to strike a blow against the pirates serving Uluch Ali, after which they could proceed to the Eastern Mediterranean. But that suggestion also received no response from the king.

Don Juan, Colonna, Solanzo, and Santa Cruz did manage to hold a war council where they agreed to leave port on the fourteenth of June.

Two days before the determined departure date, however, Don Juan suddenly announced an indefinite delay.

Colonna and Solanzo were taken aback by this and pressed him for a reason. At first the supreme commander gave no explanation, but finally hinted that the decision had come from Philip II.

Don Juan himself could not fathom what was going through the king's mind or why he would issue the order at such a time. Nevertheless, the young royal handed over the command of nine of his Spanish ships to Colonna, allowing them to sail with the Venetian fleet to the Eastern Mediterranean. Don Juan said he would remain in Messina to make preparations to attack Algiers.

Colonna responded that nine ships were not enough and asked Don Juan for twenty-five. Colonna had hoped that invoking the authority of the Pope would bring the Spanish king around, but one couldn't expect much from this strategy since the new Pope had only recently been installed. Don Juan consulted with his Spanish advisors and consented to the loan of 22 war galleys, 1,000 Spanish soldiers, and 4,000 Italian soldiers.

With 22 Spanish ships, 12 ships from the Papal States, 25 Venetian ships led by Solanzo, and the 75 Venetian ships waiting in Corfu, the fleet totaled 134 ships. There were also the six galleasses, and after adding the ships from Crete, the allied fleet topped out at over 150 ships. Although that year's force was inferior compared to the 200-plus ships they had used at Lepanto, they were certainly strong enough to take on the Turkish fleet.

They decided to set out for the Eastern Mediterranean in search of the enemy. 15 of the Spanish ships would follow somewhat behind the rest of the fleet because they needed to pick up soldiers along the way. For the time being, at least, the Venetians must have felt a sense of relief.

On July 15th they arrived in Corfu, where they joined the 75 Venetian ships led by the Venetian navy's commander in chief, Foscarini. The combined fleet left Corfu and followed the Peloponnesian peninsula south, rounded the tip, and set an eastbound course. A dispatch ship caught up with them, however, and brought news that Don Juan had left Messina with the remaining ships. Philip II had revoked his earlier order.

Colonna and the Venetian commanders discussed whether to return to Corfu to wait for Don Juan so that they could set out together for the Eastern Mediterranean. The alternative was to keep the fleet on course while sending a message back to Don Juan requesting that he catch up. Now that the fleet was on its way, the Venetians didn't want to lose a perfectly good opportunity by returning to base, especially not to a base like Corfu, which was safer and had better facilities than the one in Messina. Who knew when the chance to leave port would come again? Colonna felt the same way. The ships continued eastward after dispatching a message to Supreme Commander Don Juan.

The fleet stopped on August 4th at the island of Cerigo, a Venetian holding near the southern tip of the Peloponnesian peninsula.

They had received word that the 160-ship Turkish fleet led by Uluch Ali was in the harbor of Malvasia. Since a ship could travel there and back in one day, the Christian fleet decided on a battle formation.

As at Lepanto, they used a composite formation, mixing together ships from different nations. The ships this year, however, were so overwhelmingly Venetian that they decided to put them into groups of five: three ships from Venice with one from Spain and one from the Papal States. The main force would once again assemble in the center around Colonna's ship, fortified on his left by Commander in Chief Foscarini of the Venetian fleet and on his right by Commander Don Andrade of the Spanish fleet. There was no other choice but to assign command of the left and right flanks to Venetian captains. The mercenary Doria, whose behavior the previous year had aroused a great deal of suspicion, was not a part of this year's fleet.

Uluch Ali, meanwhile, was monitoring the Christian fleet and had decided not to venture out of the harbor of Malvasia for the time being. He actually didn't set out until August 10th. Even then, neither side seemed intent on a full-scale battle; there was only a brief skirmish, with the Turks incurring most of the damage. Seven of their galleys were rendered unusable and were abandoned. Uluch Ali then withdrew all his forces back into the harbor.

At this point Colonna had a sudden change of heart and insisted that, since Don Juan must already have reached Corfu, the fleet should withdraw to rendezvous with him, either in Corfu or somewhere between there and their current location. His reasoning was that Uluch Ali was a veteran pirate who knew the Mediterranean inside and out; it would be child's play for him to elude the main body of the allied fleet and attack Don Juan's column of fifty-odd ships, so they had to rush to Don Juan's defense before that happened.

The Venetian captains were strongly opposed, but this time Sebastiano Veniero wasn't there to physically intimidate the small, delicately-built Colonna, who would have cowered like a dove under the verbal abuse of the eagle Veniero.

Colonna insisted that he had been granted command authority for the fleet until they rejoined Don Juan. The affable Venetian admiral Foscarini, Veniero's polar opposite, yielded to Colonna's demands. The fleet had the enemy in its sights but decided to retreat.

They left Cerigo Island and headed north around the Peloponnesian peninsula. They reached the island of Zante but still hadn't caught sight of Don Juan. There was no choice but to continue northward, and they were only able to join up with Don Juan when they reached Corfu.

Don Juan was enraged that they hadn't waited for him. He threatened to execute Don Andrade, commander of the Spanish contingent. He furthermore demanded that Spanish soldiers be stationed on Venetian ships. The Venetians firmly refused. They had acquiesced to this demand the previous year, when the Venetian ships were understaffed, but this year they already had plenty of manpower.

Don Juan's demand was rooted not in reason but in vanity. His position and authority as supreme commander had gone to his head. He responded with anger when the Venetians refused. Colonna felt caught in the middle and suggested a compromise whereby the soldiers on the Papal States' ships would be moved to the Venetian ships and Spanish soldiers would take their places on the papal ships. The Venetian admiral accepted Colonna's solution.

Such games hadn't been necessary the previous year. To begin with, "The Fortress" Veniero never relented no matter what Don Juan did or how upset he became, instead showering the angry Don Juan and the perplexed Colonna with abuse and then storming out of the room. It was Barbarigo who stayed behind to settle what had to be settled, something he did calmly, logically, but also without budging an inch.

The leadership of 1572, however, didn't have this "fire and water" combination that had worked to such marvelous effect the year before. The Venetian commander didn't consider things deeply, could barely see past his own nose, and by giving in to Don Juan established a precedent that led only to further compromise. In this sense, the Venetian fleet of 1572 was an extension of the Venetian government of 1572.

Colonna's idea may have held the fleet together, but the time spent arguing had been wasted. It was ten days before the allied fleet set out once again on the Ionian Sea. The nimble admiral Uluch Ali, however, was long gone. Bad luck in the form of poor weather also diminished any hopes of victory. No one objected when Don Juan ordered them back to Corfu after having lost all prospect of actually spotting the enemy. Thereafter, the Christian and Muslim fleets only engaged in a series of small-scale skirmishes between their reconnaissance squadrons.

Don Juan returned to Messina leading his Spanish fleet, and Colonna set out for Rome. King Philip II sent a letter to the Pope promising to provide an even more powerful fleet the following year, but the Venetians no longer believed him. Lacking faith in Spain, the Venetians decided to conduct their own private negotiations with the Turks. Ambassador Barbaro, stationed in Constantinople, received a top-secret directive to that end from the Council of Ten.

The peace negotiations had to be conducted in absolute secrecy. Venice, Spain, and the Papal States had agreed in the Holy League charter that none of them would agree to a peace treaty with the Turks without first informing the other two. The Venetian Republic may have lost faith in its allies, but that didn't change the fact that it was in violation of this agreement.

Since it was necessary to proceed in secrecy even within the Venetian homeland, the question was not offered for discussion in the senate, the public forum for foreign affairs. This was a matter for the Council of Ten, known for its absolute secrecy and capacity for swift decision-making.

Though peace negotiations were never easy, there was in this case the additional issue of betraying the alliance. Absolute secrecy being of the essence, the Venetian government assembled an expanded session of the Council of Ten. The normal Council of Ten consisted of ten councilors and the doge, along with his six deputies, tallying seventeen in all. All members were noblemen over thirty who held seats in the senate. As many as twenty noblemen composed a group called the *zonta* and could be added to the first seventeen to establish a combined thirty-seven-member expanded Council of Ten. This was sanctioned under Venetian law in cases where the decisions made could determine the fate of the republic. The twenty selected for the *zonta* were men with experience in foreign and military affairs, and each was technically eligible for inclusion in the normal Council of Ten, the most powerful executive organ in the Venetian republican system.

According to Venetian law, the ten councilors of the Council of Ten and the doge's deputies had to stand for annual reelection. In times of dire emergency, however, such a frequent turnover of leadership was not only inefficient but detrimental to consistent policy making. Yet the foundational principle of the Venetian government, intended to prevent the accumulation of power in any individual's hands, was the regular transfer of that power. Such a policy could not simply be changed.

The *zonta* system came into being as a response to this uniquely Venetian situation. Though councilors would lose their position in the Council of Ten after six months, they could still participate in high-level decision-making by becoming members of the *zonta*. By the same token, members of the *zonta* could be reelected to the council. This system allowed Venetian policy to remain consistent throughout a crisis and also saved time since everyone involved in the discussions already knew all the pertinent details.

The Council of Ten and *zonta* of 1572 ordered the Venetian ambassador to Constantinople to reopen peace negotiations with the Turks regarding control of Cyprus. The Venetians wanted the island reverted to them in return for a massive increase in the 8,000-ducat annual tribute Venice paid to the Ottoman Empire before war broke out. The expanded Council of Ten voted to send Barbaro a 50,000-ducat secret discretionary fund to use during the talks. Bribery was a common tool in negotiations with the ministers of the Turkish court.

The Council of Ten and the *zonta* also sought to involve the French in their peace negotiations. Their effort was aided by the French king's animosity towards the Spanish and his strong desire to drive a wedge between Venice and Spain. The negotiations in Constantinople continued on several parallel fronts: Barbaro met with Grand Vizier Sokullu, Sokullu met with the French ambassador, and the French ambassador met with Barbaro.

The Turks may have lost the Battle of Lepanto, but negotiating with them was far from easy. The Turks understood full well that Spain was unreliable and that Venice could do nothing on its own. The Ottoman Empire's "beard" was shaved off at Lepanto, but thanks to Uluch Ali's dedication it had grown back. The Turks were again full of confidence. Barbaro, on the other hand, was quite distressed. His only hope was that the Turks' memory of their defeat at Lepanto would bring them to the table despite their outward display of self-assurance.

With the resumption of negotiations, the boards were taken off the windows of the Venetian embassy in

Pera. The Janissary guard also left. At least the exterior of the building no longer looked like the legation of an enemy power.

It was no surprise that the negotiations didn't go smoothly. After all, Cyprus was now firmly in Turkish hands. One couldn't reasonably expect the Turks simply to hand it back even for a substantial increase in the annual tribute payments.

It was also impossible, however, for Venice to accept an agreement that would force them to abandon Cyprus. Although the two bases of Nafplion and Malvasia on the Peloponnesian peninsula had been abandoned after the Battle of Preveza thirty-four years earlier, in military and economic importance those two could hardly compare to Cyprus.

With neither side willing to compromise, there was little chance that peace negotiations would make any progress.

The nearly forty members of the Council of Ten and *zonta* didn't feel comfortable making such a momentous decision alone, so they considered sending the question to the senate; at least, then, there would be two hundred people responsible for making the decision. Yet only two members voted to do so. The remaining members clearly felt that maintaining the absolute secrecy of this deliberation was of greater importance.

On November 19th, with the negotiations completely stalled, the extended Council of Ten finally sent an order to the ambassador in Constantinople telling him not to ask for the return of Cyprus. There had been another vote to send the matter to the senate before the order was sent, but that still only made three votes.

With this new mandate in hand, Ambassador Barbaro once again waded into the difficult negotiations. The old diplomat braced himself against the winds blowing across the Bosphorus from the Black Sea—the winter had turned quite severe. Despite Turkey's defeat at the Battle of Lepanto, the anti-Western hardliners in the Ottoman court grew more influential by the day.

Venice – Spring 1573

On March 7, 1573, the negotiations were finally settled and formalized. The terms, however, were so unfavorable to Venice that one is dumbfounded that these were the gains of a victor.

Cyprus was officially recognized as Turkish territory, so there was no longer a need to pay the annual tribute. Yet the Venetians still had to pay something called a "commerce fee" of 300,000 ducats within the following three years. The yearly tribute for the island of Zante had also been raised from the previous 500 to 1,000 ducats.

In exchange, the Turks would return property confiscated from Venetians living on Turkish-controlled land and grant the Venetians a guarantee of total freedom of economic activity within all Ottoman territory. The resulting peace lasted seventy-two years, until 1645. The concessions made by Venice in 1573 and all the blood spilled at the Battle of Lepanto conferred at least this much upon the people of Venice—seven decades of peace, and the economic prosperity that accompanied it.

The treaty between Venice and the Turks was made public only after it was signed. The Venetian senate itself only learned of it a day before it was made public. Even after the allied fleet had disbanded the previous October, the Venetian state shipyards were launching warships on nearly a daily basis, and crewmen were being recruited to serve on them. Until the treaty was made public, other countries and the citizens of Venice itself believed, with no reason to think otherwise, that the republic intended to continue the war.

The announcement was met with thunderous condemnation from every country in Western Europe. A single-peace treaty of this kind, they said, was a betrayal of Christendom. Yet, not a single country actually suggested that they form another fleet—this time without Venice—to fight the Turks.

By establishing a separate peace with the Turks, Venice was also able to avoid a messy entanglement in the power struggle then going on among the major powers of Europe. France and Spain both had their eye on North Africa, particularly Algiers, and this was a source of open hostility. Furthermore, by cooperating with the Turks, Venice could contain Spain's territorial ambitions in the Mediterranean.

There were also meetings underway in Constantinople between the French ambassador and the Turkish court. The two sides agreed for the French army to invade Flanders at the same time that the Turks launched an armada of three hundred galleys into the Mediterranean to attack Spanish territory. For the latter to become feasible, a wedge had to be driven between Venice and Spain, and the Turkish-Venetian alliance did just that, leaving Spain completely isolated.

Venice would play along with these French machinations but hardly allow themselves to become open enemies of Spain. The single-peace treaty with the Ottomans allowed them to survive by being neither ally nor foe of both Spain and France, the two great Western European powers in the sixteenth century.

After concluding the treaty, Venice turned its attention to reestablishing its mercantile network, particularly in the waters of the Eastern Mediterranean. This is not to say that Venice would neglect its navy. Its previous carelessness in this regard was precisely what had made it vulnerable to pressure from the territorially expansive states surrounding it. The Venetians made October 7th a state holiday to remind themselves of the glory of the Venetian navy, not just to commemorate the joy of a single victory.

Even the English, far removed from the Mediterranean, got caught up in the frenzy of excitement that rose up around the Battle of Lepanto, which turned out to be not only the largest battle fought between galleys, but also the last. It was also the final battle fought in the name of the cross. No one in Western Europe would call again for a crusade.

Western Europe became the center of the world; the Mediterranean's leading role on the stage of history came to an end. The historically decisive naval battles were henceforth fought not in the Mediterranean Sea but in the Atlantic Ocean. The era of the galley was replaced by the era of the sailing ship.

A fierce twenty-five-year war broke out in 1645

between the Venetians and the Turks over the island of Crete. By this time, however, the Mediterranean had already been pushed to the margins of the world stage, and the war was not viewed as the historic event that the Battle of Lepanto had been. No matter how long the war stretched out or how fiercely it was fought, it was just another local conflict.

The Republic of Venice had enjoyed a proud thousand-year history. The Ottoman Empire had been a major historical force since the fall of the Byzantine Empire in 1453. The Battle of Lepanto, however, set both of them on the path to decline. This was due not only to their declining power, but also to the declining importance of the Mediterranean Sea—the center of their activity and influence—as the sixteenth century came to a close.

The clearest evidence of the Mediterranean's waning importance is that all of the important sea battles that subsequently took place took place somewhere else.

The allies' military gains at the Battle of Lepanto were completely eradicated by the collapse of the alliance the following year.

Nonetheless, the tremendous amount of blood shed in the battle was certainly not shed in vain.

If the Turks had been victorious at Lepanto, their reputation for invincibility would have been reaffirmed and the Mediterranean would have turned into the inland sea of the Ottoman Empire. It is also questionable whether the Turkish drive into the European continent could have been halted at Vienna.

The after-effects of the Battle of Lepanto were more psychological than substantive, but history has demonstrated to us time and again the importance of such psychological effects. Venice, at any rate, was able to enjoy seventy years of peace, with the result that it was, during that time, one of the wealthiest and most elegant countries in Europe. The works of art and traditional handicrafts that were brought out in seemingly endless streams to impress distinguished foreign visitors during holiday processions in San Marco Piazzo were estimated to be worth approximately ten million ducats.

Among the visitors astonished at Venice's wealth were those from the Far East. In 1585, fourteen years after the Battle of Lepanto, a group of four Japanese youths who had been sent by three Christian samurai leaders in Kyushu dropped by Venice as part of a Jesuit-organized mission to visit Philip II of Spain and Pope Gregory XIII.

The Warriors of Lepanto in Later Years

In May of 1572, Pope Pius V passed away with memories of the victory at Lepanto still fresh in his mind, and before the alliance of that year disbanded without ever going to battle. Not long afterward he would be canonized as Saint Pius.

His call for a crusade and its success were the reasons for his canonization. In the thirteenth century, King Louis of France had organized a number of crusades all of which ended in failure; his efforts nevertheless resulted in his elevation to sainthood. In Western Europe, sainthood and the battle against the infidel were clearly thought to be intertwined.

Don Juan's good fortune ended after the Battle of Lepanto. The animosity between him and Philip II only worsened and he led an undistinguished life until 1578, when he died at the age of thirty-three. He never married.

Marcantonio Colonna also completely disappeared from history after Lepanto. He served as Governor General of Sicily in 1577, only to die in 1584 at age forty-nine, far from home, in Spain.

The widely criticized Gian Andrea Doria continued working as a mercenary sea captain until his death in 1606 at age sixty-seven. The waning importance of the Mediterranean meant that none of his heirs ever achieved any degree of importance.

Perhaps as a compensation for his dismissal as admiral of the Venetian fleet, Sebastiano Veniero was selected as doge of the Venetian Republic six years after the Battle of Lepanto. There were few problems with the Turks during his tenure, so he probably wasn't afforded many opportunities to lose his volatile temper.

To commemorate the four hundredth anniversary of the Battle of Lepanto, the Italian navy fastened a marble plaque to the wall of his modest house facing Formosa Square, identifying it as the home of a triumphant naval commander.

After the ratification of the peace treaty with the Turks, Venetian Ambassador to Constantinople Marcantonio Barbaro was allowed to return home after a tour lasting five years. It was customary for a returning ambassador to make a report to the senate; his report was a scathing criticism of the government's policy, one that made the assembled senators and the administration go pale with mortification:

The stability and durability of a state does not depend solely on military might. It also depends on how other states view you, and on the resolve with which you face those other states.

For several years, the Turks have sensed that we Venetians inevitably take the easy path of compromise. This is because our attitude towards them has not been one of the requisite diplomatic courtesy, but rather one of servility. We have refrained from pointing out Turkish weaknesses and have neglected to demonstrate our own strengths.

As a result, the Turks can no longer suppress their intrinsic haughtiness, insolence, and arrogance; they can give their irrational passions free rein. We allowed them to take Cyprus in return for a scrap of a letter delivered by a minor functionary, a subjugated Greek no less. What is this if not proof of the shame of Venetian foreign policy?

Even after such a report, the Venetian government didn't fail to reward him for all his accomplishments. He soon received a position of honor second only to the doge when he was appointed the director of the San Marco Cathedral.

Ambassador plenipotentiaries were under no similar obligation to report to the senate upon their return. As noted earlier, Barbaro's colleague Giovanni Solanzo was immediately sent out to sea in 1572 to replace Barbarigo as admiral in the Venetian fleet. Four years later, while leading a patrol squadron on a voyage through the Mediterranean, he ended up in a skirmish with some ships belonging to the Maltese Order of the Knights of St. John. He was killed during that action. The Order was furious at Venice for signing a treaty with the Turks, and thereafter attacked Venetian ships as if they belonged to the infidel Turks themselves.

Uluch Ali lived to the ripe old age of seventy-five. He died in bed in Constantinople in 1595. In my collection *Chronicles of Love*, there is a story entitled "The Emerald Sea" that treats an episode from Uluch Ali's romantic life.

There was a rumor, even during the Battle of Lepanto, about a plot by King Philip II of Spain to win Uluch Ali over. It seems the king actually attempted this at some later date. The former Christian from southern Italy, however, never betrayed the Turks, who valued him enough to appoint him grand admiral of their navy. He spent his personal fortune erecting a beautiful mosque in Constantinople to which he donated many treasures, and died peacefully in his sleep, a Muslim to the end. During his own lifetime, it is said, he never allowed the Venetian navy even a moment of sleep.

Venice – Winter 1571

The Venetian government forbade those who had lost loved ones at Lepanto to wear attires of mourning. This was to be a time of celebration, not of grief. Festival flags flew everywhere on the streets, while not a single black flag was hoisted. The doge and high officials of the Venetian Republic visited Agostino Barbarigo's residence, not to offer their condolences but rather to celebrate the victory. His widow, who also wasn't wearing mourning clothes, received them with stoic composure. The exaltation of victory, rather than grief over the loss of loved ones, was the reigning emotion in the entire city, even in the Barbarigo manor.

There was one woman in Venice who shut herself off to mourning, in both body and mind, more than everybody else. She wouldn't have been able to wear mourning clothes in any event, since she was formally in no position to mourn anyone.

She hadn't even set foot in the church that contained the Barbarigo family crypt. She knew that the only thing entombed there was a lock of Agostino's hair, but that wasn't the reason. She hesitated to visit his tomb because she felt that doing so would render his death no different from all deaths.

The commotion of the victory celebrations outside was nothing more to her than noise; it had nothing to do with her. She could understand why victory may have been a joyous occasion to others, but she couldn't share in the joy.

Her old maidservant knew that she had been too stunned to cry when news of the victory at Lepanto came together with that of her beloved's death, but could only be considerate and nothing more. Flora, having nobody to whom she could confide her sadness, locked it away deep within her heart.

She still had a few of his belongings. These were not things he had left behind as mementoes, but rather articles the two of them had used in the small house he had rented for her. There was delicate Venetian glassware and a glass carafe for wine. There were also shirts, tablecloths and napkins adorned with wispy cloudlike lace, and other such odds and ends.

The day after she heard of his death, she went to that house and brought those things back home. After that, she would never be able to visit the place, which was rented in his name.

She had one other thing of his: on a certain chilly night when he had been escorting her home, he wrapped her in his cloak. It was the normal outerwear for Venetian men at the time, black wool with a fur lining. Just wearing that cloak gave her a certain peace of mind, as if she were surrounded by his love.

Her sadness was profound, but she didn't feel alone. Once a woman is loved by a man with all his heart, she will never again suffer from abject loneliness. True, she found herself pining for something that she couldn't reach, but that was that. She would steep herself in that feeling for as long as it lasted, she told herself; she wouldn't fight it.

Though she wouldn't visit the Barbarigo family crypt, she did not give up her habit of visiting the Church of San Zaccaria with her son in the afternoons, when there was no one else around. She prayed for Agostino there.

She did not, however, pray for him to rest in peace. He had died with the knowledge of victory. She had no doubt he had died fulfilled.

On one of those afternoons, she exited the Church of San Zaccaria after finishing her prayers and came to a halt in front of a typical Venetian cistern near the middle of the square. The peaceful sunlight of the winter afternoon had made her stop without realizing it. She closed her eyes and tilted her head slightly towards the sky, as if to receive the sunlight.

She felt an arm gently wrap around her back. Her son was beside her. "Mother, he died the commander of a victorious battle."

She was startled and looked at him. She had thought of him only as a child, and yet he understood what was in her heart. She was also surprised at how high on her back his arm was—he had certainly grown a great deal during the past year or two. His voice was also deeper, and calmer.

She couldn't help but smile. All this time she had

viewed him as a child, but now he was old enough to be comforting her. The realization was actually more amusing than pleasing. It really was true how they grew up right before your eyes at that age. He had been like a puppy following her around, but now he was about to turn thirteen. In two or three years, he'd have to decide whether to learn the arts of navigation and commerce through practical experience as a crossbowman on a merchant ship, or study law or medicine at the University in Padua. Seven years from now, when he turned twenty, he would be granted a seat in the assembly of the Republic, as the heir of a Venetian aristocrat. He would still need his mother for the next seven or, at most, ten years.

"Mother, let's go to Corfu someday."

She nodded.

She looked at her son, whose head was now above her own.

"Perhaps it is I who need him," Flora thought. Tears welled up in her eyes and rolled down her cheeks for the first time since the day she heard the news.

They departed San Zaccaria, the son's left arm around his mother. Flora bought a tiny potted flower from the woman who was always there selling flowers she brought in from the countryside. The woman told Flora that if she took care of it, the flower would grow and bloom so profusely that in the spring she would have to change its flowerpot.

Even if her son chose to go to sea, he would never in his lifetime be menaced by the gleaming scimitar of the Turk.

Agostino Barbarigo had bequeathed a gift to the son of his beloved.

To the Reader
- In Lieu of an Epilogue -

I first read Homer's *Iliad* during the summer I was sixteen. The world was transformed right before my eyes.

It was unclear, though, exactly what within me had changed. Perhaps everything I've written in my life so far has been an attempt to answer that question, and perhaps that desire will keep pulling me forward until the day I die.

Because it was the *Iliad* that first awakened my fascination with the world of the Mediterranean, I have always been drawn to the challenge of depicting war— particularly those wars that represent, as in the *Iliad*, confrontations between different civilizations. There were only three such wars in the Mediterranean during the Renaissance, which is my period of expertise: the fall of Constantinople in 1453, the siege of Rhodes in 1522, and the Battle of Lepanto in 1571.

Much to the misfortune of the people living in those times, many battles besides these three also took place. But in terms of historical importance—in other words, that something actually *changed* because of them— these three battles are particularly noteworthy.

This is not to say that I decided to write about these three conflicts that summer when I turned sixteen. The idea wasn't even in my mind when I wrote my first book, *Women of the Renaissance*, more than ten years later. I think the idea first occurred to me a full twenty-five years later, when I was working on my comprehensive history of the Venetian Republic, *A Tale of the City of the Sea.*

The Fall of Constantinople and *The Battle of Lepanto* directly concern the Venetian Republic. *The Siege of Rhodes* could not have been written without Venetian historical documents. The detailed and objective records that still survive in Venice taught me a great deal about these three battles that changed history, and the narratives started to take shape within my mind. This provided me with the perfect opportunity to fulfill the ardent wish I had nursed since that summer I was sixteen: to write about war in the Mediterranean. Writing *A Tale of the City of the Sea* was what made it possible for me to write this Mediterranean trilogy.

I read Homer's *Iliad* many times, thinking there must be something that I could take from it, but other than the central theme of humanity itself there was almost nothing to appropriate. Much of that work deals with the delightful idea of the gods divided into opposing cheering sections, with Athena and others rooting for the Greeks, and Poseidon and his squad supporting the Trojans. This is a very enjoyable element of the story, but totally inappropriate for a work set in the Renaissance. I therefore abandoned the idea.

Another inimitable aspect of the *Iliad* is that it begins during the tenth year of a ten-year war. The more I thought about this, the more painfully apparent it became just what a genius Homer really was, and just how impossible it would be to imitate him. The defense of Constantinople, the capital of the Eastern Roman Empire, lasted about fifty days, the siege of Rhodes about six months, while the Battle of Lepanto was decided in under five hours. No matter how impressive I found the Homeric technique, I simply couldn't use it. Beginning the *Iliad* during the tenth year is effective precisely because the war had dragged on for ten years.

In the end, I depicted each of these three conflicts in the ways that I thought would be most appropriate, whether it be for a fifty-day war or a six-month siege. In the case of the five-hour Battle of Lepanto, I tried to create a crescendo leading up to the battle, and a decrescendo gliding down from its conclusion.

I have not included a bibliography in any of the individual works or for the trilogy as a whole. My most important reference sources were listed in the appendix to *A Tale of the City of the Sea Continued*, which should give some idea of how essential the research done for two volumes of Venetian history was to the inception of the present trilogy. As I continue to read Venice's extant archival papers, I feel even more strongly that nothing is more effective in appealing to later generations than to leave an accurate and objective record.

Florence, Spring 1987

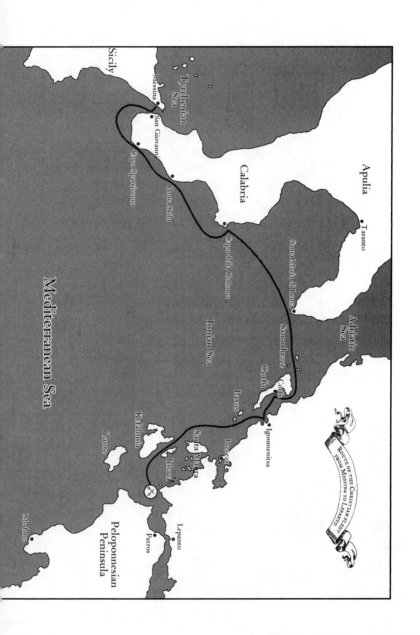

ROUTE OF THE CHRISTIAN FLEET FROM MESSINA TO LEPANTO

Sicily

Messina

San Giovanni

Capo Spartivento

Punta Stilo

Tyrrhenian Sea

Calabria

Apulia

Taranto

Capo della Colonna

Santa Maria di Leuca

Adriatic Sea

Ionian Sea

Mediterranean Sea

Samothrace

Corfu

Corfu

Paxos

Igoumenitsa

Zante

Kefalonia

Santa Maura

Preveza

Ithaca

Modone

Peloponnesian Peninsula

Patros

Lepanto

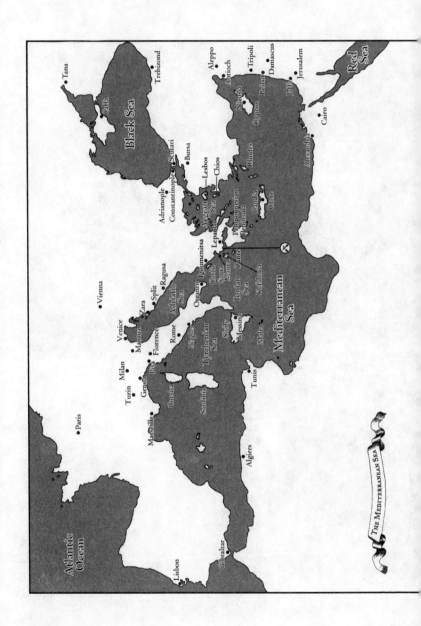

The Mediterranean Sea